Brant's *voice* ___ and
pulled her bac___

"I don't think your adopting Annie is such a good idea."

"Of all the. . .I can't believe. . ." was all she managed as she stormed back into the room.

"Look," he said, "I know it's none of my business, but—"

"It's one thing to overhear a private conversation, Mr. McCourt. It's an altogether different thing to think you've got a right to get involved in it!"

Brant sat up. Mocking her formality, he said, "Miss Stern, would it be possible for you to cut me some slack? If you really want a reason to be mad at me I can give you one, but if you could just give me one minute. . ."

"Did it occur to you that I might not be interested in listening to your opinion about my future?"

"Just who *are* you listening to these days? Seems to me you don't hear much beyond your own voice."

"How dare you!"

Brant shoved one foot into a boot and said, "I dare because I've been there, Miss Stern! I think you've got your own interests in mind here and not what's best for that little girl!"

Paige gripped the back of a chair. Never in her adult life had she had such a conversation with a virtual stranger. "You've been hanging around here for one week and already you're an expert on the residents' welfare and mine, too? What do you know about Annie, and what could you possibly know about me?"

BECKY MELBY AND CATHY WIENKE made their
Heartsong Presents debut with the contemporary
novel, *Beauty for Ashes*. Becky has won several
awards for her short fiction, while Cathy, an avid quilter
and reader, is just beginning to pursue her interest in
writing. Both are active in their churches, and both
have children of various ages.

Books by Becky Melby and Cathy Wienke

HEARTSONG PRESENTS
HP98—Beauty for Ashes
HP169—Garment of Praise

Far Above Rubies

Becky Melby
Cathy Wienke

Heartsong Presents

To Brian and our son Michael,
my two paramedics,
and to Michael's beloved
Rebecca Humphreys Wienke.
Cathy

To Bill, my very own pilot and my very best friend.
Becky

A note from the Author:
*I love to hear from my readers! You may write to me at
the following address:* **Becky Melby & Cathy Wienke**
Author Relations
P.O. Box 719
Uhrichsville, OH 44683

ISBN 1-57748-194-1

FAR ABOVE RUBIES

Cover illustration by Lorraine Bush.

PRINTED IN THE U.S.A.

one

Paige's foot kept time to the music as she pumped the pedal that turned the potter's wheel. Chubby little fingers slid beneath hers on the slick, wet clay. Paige looked up at the mirror and laughed at the wide-eyed expression of the little girl on her lap. Their creation was getting taller and skinnier by the second.

"Annie, are we making a vase or a giraffe?"

Annie's dark brown ringlets bounced as she giggled. "Raf! Make raf!"

"Okay, Sweet Stuff, giraffe it is!" Paige said as she took her foot off the pedal. "But we have to stop now or the poor giraffe won't be able to hold his head up."

"No stop!" Annie's fingertips dug into the thinning tower of clay as it was slowing down. Suddenly, the top half collapsed and thudded onto the table. Paige held her breath, bracing for another temper tantrum, hoping this would be one of the times that she'd be able to distract Annie and ward off her easily-triggered anger. She picked up the broken piece and handed it to Annie. Annie took it, glared at it, looked for a moment like she might throw it across the room, and then began to laugh. "Raf's head falled off! Silly raf!"

"Silly giraffe!" Paige kissed the top of Annie's head and laughed with her, more out of relief than anything. She looked up at the clock. "It's supper time. Should we wash up now?"

"Eat now!" Annie slid off her lap and ran toward the door of the occupational therapy room.

"Annie! Look at your hands!" Paige's warning came a split second after Annie's left hand flattened against the window and her right grabbed the handle of the locked door. "Look at your hands!" Paige repeated.

The little girl held up her hands as if seeing them for the first time. "Yuch-y!"

"Very yuchy!" Paige stepped on the bar that turned on the water at the half-circle sink. "Let's wash and then we can eat."

Annie giggled again as spots of dried clay on the backs of her hands turned dark, then disappeared under the spray.

Pulling a paper towel from the dispenser, Paige handed one to her. "Wonder what's for supper," she said.

"Don-odes."

"Not today. Tomorrow we're going to McDonald's with Hailey, and then we're going to buy a new dress for Hailey's wedding and go to the zoo and—"

"DON-ODES!" The wadded paper towel hit the sink.

"I think I smell spaghetti!"

"DON-ODES! NOW!" Two small rubber-soled shoes slapped the vinyl floor. Two hands opened and closed, looking for something to throw.

Paige bent down and picked up the slight-built three-year-old and wrapped her in her arms. "Sunshine and rain," she whispered. "So many smiles and so many tears."

There were no commands to stop the tears, just a gentle restraint, a technique taught her by one of the physical therapists. Since self-control was sometimes impossible for children with Fetal Alcohol Syndrome, there were times when the boundaries of loving arms gave them the security of knowing they wouldn't be able to cause harm.

Annie's fists beat against her, but she didn't try to squirm out of her arms. She vented and then grew still, rubbing her wet cheeks on Paige's shoulder. After a minute she looked up and smiled, her eyes sparkling and her dimples deepening.

"You yike sketti, Paige?" she asked.

"I love sketti, and I love you."

Planting a noisy kiss on Paige's cheek, Annie said, "I yuv you, too."

Paige walked slowly to the full-length mirror. Annie's arms and legs were wrapped around her neck and waist, and Paige smiled at their reflection. Three months ago, on a Friday night, she would have been dining al fresco at a sidewalk café or sipping café au lait and listening to music with other art students at an all-night bistro. If someone had given her a preview back then of the thoughts she was thinking today, she would have laughed. But three months ago she was in Paris.

At times she wondered if she would lose herself in this small Wisconsin town. She loved what her brother had started here at the Sparrow Center; from the beginning she had written to him faithfully about it, encouraging him when the project seemed in danger of being sabotaged. David needed something to throw himself into; that's how God blessed him, because that was David's sort of thing. He had always been the one with the tender heart and the desire for order and predictability. Paige, on the other hand, had always been the one with the longing to see the world, the craving for adventure, the one who thrived on change.

Two years ago, when David was still working on the blueprints for the Sparrow Center, she had volunteered to paint murals on the Center walls—but never in her wildest dreams had she seen herself living here in Milbrooke. Even a year ago, when David and Karlee were planning their wedding and the idea of moving in with Karlee's sister, Hailey Austin, had first come up, she'd seen it as a temporary thing. Living in Karlee's rustic log home was just one more adventure, a chance to experience life in the Midwest. . .for a while.

So how, she wondered, had she reached so quickly the point she was at now? Her life had become filled with her work with handicapped children, fingerpaint and papier mâché, and trips to the zoo. How had it happened?

She stared at her hand against Annie's back, at the pearl ring on her little finger. She hadn't taken it off in five years, maybe she never would. It was there to keep her sights high, to remind her never to settle for less than the best. Five years ago, even three months ago, what she held now in her arms would not have seemed like the best—but then the one thing she had wanted to avoid at all cost was predictability. Little Annie, though, craved the security of predictability; it was one of the things she needed most.

Annie laid her head against her shoulder, and Paige continued to study their reflection. Her own hair was sleek and straight and curved under just below her chin, but it was only a shade darker than Annie's and their eyes were the same deep brown. Annie's skin was darker, but that would only be a problem for those who chose to make it one.

"We look pretty good together, don't we, Annie-kins?" she said.

At twenty-eight and single, Paige Stern was trying on the name "Mommy" for the first time—and she liked the fit.

≈

The call came in to the Sparrow Children's Center at 5:46 P.M. Karen Jonas, the second-shift receptionist, answered the phone.

"Yes, I was wondering if the executive director might still be in?"

"He's at dinner right now, may I take a message?"

"Yes. . .this is Warren Klug, attorney for Roman Slayder. . ."

Karen's eyes widened. The name would have meant nothing to her if she hadn't just been reading about him two days earlier while standing in line at the grocery store. But what in the world did Robert Worth, their executive director, have to do with Roman Slayder? She took a quick breath and tried to find her professional voice again. "Dr. Worth is just down the hall, Mr. Klug. Can you hold while I get him?"

"Yes. Thank you."

Karen skidded to a stop in front of the break room where Robert Worth was talking with Paige and several employees over pie and coffee. "Phone!" was the only word she could get out.

Robert looked at her with a patiently amused expression. "For whom, Karen?"

"For you! Long distance!" She lowered her voice to a conspiratorial whisper. "It's Roman Slayder's lawyer!" When Robert didn't jump out of his chair, she added, "Do you know who Roman Slayder is?"

Standing up casually, Robert said, "No, I don't."

"He's the lead singer for Quaestor!" She grimaced and almost shivered at the name of the heavy-metal rock band.

"Mm-hm." Robert smiled and picked up his plate. Taking another fork full of pie, he said, "Don't bother me until the president calls, Miss Jonas."

"I'm serious!"

This time, the look on her face convinced him. Wiping his mouth with his napkin, Robert cleared his throat, decided against using the phone in the break room, and walked down the hall to his office. After listening and nodding for several minutes, Robert finally asked a question, to which Mr. Klug replied, "I'm not saying that my client is denying paternity, Dr. Worth, only that there is naturally some cause for doubt. He's willing to have the blood test done and, if the results do not rule out the possibility of his involvement, he would like to see the child."

"Yes. Of course. Are you free to tell me what his intentions are if it is determined that he is Anika's father? Now that the mother has finally decided to release her for adoption—"

"I can tell you honestly," Mr. Klug interrupted, "that I do not believe he would consider relinquishing his rights. But, of course. . .there is the concern. . .we know, of course, that she has Fetal Alcohol Syndrome, but just how. . .um. . .severe is her case? What is her prognosis?"

Robert rubbed a hand over tired eyes. He'd had a long day, and this was not the first question of this nature he'd had to deal with in the past twelve hours. If only he had the answers. "Anika is a very special little girl, Mr. Klug. She has been diagnosed with Fetal Alcohol Effects, which is less severe than FAS. Her speech is somewhat delayed, she is still in diapers at night, and she has a very short attention span. We know that she will always struggle with learning disabilities, but it is too early to determine just how severe. She is very outgoing, but social and emotional dysfunction in these children tends to escalate in the teen years, so it is very difficult to predict what the future holds."

Robert sighed. "Anika has had a very hard life; she's been in and out of foster homes. Mr. Klug, a stable environment is essential to the well-being of these children."

"Are you implying that my client cannot furnish a stable environment for his own child?"

Robert rolled his eyes. *This guy must be great in court,* he thought. Taking a deep breath and ignoring the challenge, Robert simply said, "We'll take care of the lab tests on our end. We'll be in touch with you when the results come back."

&

Two hours later, Robert picked up his briefcase, locked his office door, and walked slowly down the hall, past the nursery, and toward the residential wing. It wasn't often that he worked this late, and when he did, he loved to walk down the dimly lit corridors, stopping to peek at sleeping children or giving a word of encouragement to an employee struggling to settle a restless child. At such times, the miracle of the Sparrow Center never failed to overwhelm him again. They had been accepting residents for only ten months and already they were full and making plans for a new wing. He remembered the months of planning, when the Center had been only a vision and a prayer and gave silent praise for God's faithfulness.

This night he stopped in a doorway at the sound of a quiet voice. He looked in to see Paige sitting on the edge of the bed, her back to the door. She bent down to kiss the sleeping child. "Shelly's old room is pink," she said, "but we can paint it any color you want. And there's a barn— maybe we can get a pony when you get a little bigger." Picking up a stack of books from the floor, she whispered, "Oh, I almost forgot to tell you. . .I looked up your name at the library. Anika means 'very beautiful'."

two

It was just after 7:30 in the morning when Paige and Hailey stepped out of the car in the employee parking lot of the Sparrow Center, yet the heat shimmering off the blacktop promised a mid-summer scorcher. As Hailey touched her key to the door knob, the door opened and one of the third-shift nurses stepped out. She greeted Hailey, then smiled at Paige. The coffee-colored skin crinkled around her eyes as she said, "I sure hope your name is Paige!"

Hailey grabbed the door and held it open with her shoulder. "Must be nice to be famous! Marie, this is the celebrated artist, Paige Stern; Paige meet Marie Wassal, third shift nursing supervisor. Marie runs the tightest ship and has the softest heart in the Center."

Paige held out her hand, "Glad to meet you, Marie."

"And I'm thrilled to meet you, Paige." She nodded toward the hallway behind her. "I love your murals, but your fame goes far beyond your artwork today!"

"Oh?"

"There's a little girl in there who's been asking for you nonstop since five o'clock this morning!"

"Uh-oh."

Marie laughed. "The Lord sure knew what he was doing when He made her such a sweet thing. She's been jabbering about 'rafs' and 'yions' and monkeys all morning, but by lunchtime you may have a little terror on your hands! I'll be praying for you two!"

Paige put her hand on Hailey's shoulder. "Nurse Hailey is in charge of tantrum control today."

Hailey gave an unconvincing smile, then turned to Marie. "How's the new baby?"

"Still critical, but I think he'll be okay. Second shift did an IV Rocephin over one hour. His pulse ox is 94%, and I imagine they'll do a repeat chest film this morning, then we'll know more." Marie turned to include Paige in her answer. "Sad case; three-month-old cocaine baby with pneumonia. His mother is only fifteen. She and the grandmother didn't have a clue in the world that he was as sick as he was when they brought him in. They think we can just fix him up and they can take him home again."

"You don't think her case worker will allow that, do you?" Hailey asked.

"I hope not. Let's pray this will wake that little girl up and force her into detox. Well, you two have a lovely day. I'm going home to air-conditioning and a nice, soft bed!"

⁂

Annie sat on her knees, stabbing bites of pancake with her fork while she chattered. One of the nurses' aides had fixed her hair in corn-row braids and the pastel beads tapped together as she turned her head back and forth, taking in everything around her.

"What color dress do you want to wear for my wedding?" Hailey asked.

"Red. Or bwack. . .or lello. . ."

"How about pink?" Paige suggested.

Annie nodded vigorously, the beads clicking wildly. "I yike pink!"

Paige exchanged a look of relief with Hailey. "Okay, pink it is!"

Annie fell asleep on the drive to Milwaukee, giving her an hour nap and giving Paige the hope that her good mood could last all day. They woke her gently and cautiously when they got to the mall and Paige carried her in. Annie was ready to run as soon as she saw the waterfall in the center of the mall, but Hailey took her firmly by the hand while Paige went ahead and rented a stroller.

When Paige met up with them a few minutes later, Hailey was lifting Annie up to stare at wedding rings in a jewelry store window.

Paige held her arms out to Annie and shook her head at Hailey. "You already have one of those!"

"We're picking out one for you."

"Swell, then we'll go buy a wedding gown and pick out china and then we'll run over to Penney's and order a groom from the catalog!"

"Don't laugh! It would be just about that easy for you. All you'd have to do is stand on a street corner in Milbrooke and announce that you were ready to get married and you'd have a dozen proposals instantly!"

"Thank you for that comforting advice. And if I stand on the street corner and scream, I don't want to get married! do you think all you match-makers will leave me alone? I mean, does it say 'desperate' on my forehead or something? I got a letter from my mother yesterday telling me that she 'just happened' to run into the mother of this guy I had a crush on in eighth grade and—can you believe it?—he 'just happens' to still be single! What a strange coincidence. . .hint, hint, hint."

Annie, one stubby finger bent against the glass, said,

"Buy dat one."

Paige held up her hand and wiggled her little finger. "I already have a pretty ring."

Hailey put her finger on the glass next to Annie's. "But it's not the right kind and it's not on the right finger, is it Annie?"

With no idea what she was agreeing to, Annie shook her braids. "You need one doze wings, Paige."

Paige gave an arrogant sniff and stuck her nose in the air. "Diamonds are so. . .traditional."

"I just read an article that said that other stones are becoming really popular for engagement rings. Look at that emerald marquis, and there's a sapphire. . ."

Paige made a face and bent to put Annie in the stroller. "Annie is getting tired of looking at silly rings. Let's go find that pink dress."

As Paige buckled the belt of the stroller, Annie pointed to her pearl ring. "Dat's a pwetty wing."

Paige kissed her on the cheek. "Thank you, sweetie." Looking at Hailey as she stood up, she said, "I'm glad some people like it."

"Hey! I like it! I just don't want to think of you going through life with nothing but an antique pinky ring from a flea market!" Realizing what she'd just said, she grimaced. "I'm sorry."

Paige shook her head. "I will forgive you on one condition—that if you associate the word 'ring' or 'wedding' or 'date' or 'man' with me even once today you will voluntarily become polar bear lunch. Do we understand each other?"

"Yes, ma'am." Hailey put one hand on the handle of the stroller. "Beeper on?"

"Beeper on."

"Okay, let's go find that pink dress."

As they walked, Paige glanced down at the pearl on her finger. It was such a part of her that, though she looked at it hundreds of times a day, she seldom really saw it anymore. But once in a while the smell of burning leaves or the angle of the sun let her see it with the same eyes that had first spotted it on a dusty table cluttered with knick-knacks and gaudy costume jewelry. In those moments she was transported, if only for a fraction of a second, to an outdoor flea market on a warm September afternoon six years earlier.

For an artist with a passion for out-of-print children's books and antique jewelry, it was a place of magic. To Gavin Prentice, it might as well have been the Amazon Jungle. He had tolerated the afternoon, fitting himself into her plans because it was her last day in Milbrooke. When Paige had laughed at the exorbitant price on the ring and tried to set it down, Gavin had grabbed it from her and paid the ridiculous figure without batting an eye.

It was only their second date, and it hadn't been a day worth writing about in her journal or telling her roommate about when she got back to school. It was only months later, when she'd come to know the man behind the cool exterior, that the day, and the ring, became something to treasure.

&

In less than an hour they were driving through the gates at the zoo. Annie sat in back in her car seat, clutching the bag that held a pink gingham dress with spaghetti straps, smocked top, and layers of eyelet lace. They'd had a near-disaster when they told her she couldn't wear it to the zoo, but peace was restored when Paige handed her a nickel to throw into the fountain.

They rented a stroller again, and as they walked, Hailey pulled a tube of sunscreen from her pocket and applied it liberally to her pale arms and freckled nose. "I wish I had your skin," she sighed.

"Trade you my skin for your fiancé."

Hailey turned slowly, staring at Paige from beneath her brimmed hat. "Wait a minute! Isn't this a taboo subject?"

"Not if I bring it up."

"So, if you bring it up, do I get fed to the bears if I answer you?"

"Maybe." Paige stopped in front of the zebras and pulled a sketch pad and pencil out of her sidepack. She was having trouble with one of her murals for the Center, and she was hoping that a real, live model would inspire her. She squatted down so Annie could watch her draw. The dimples in the little girl's brown face deepened as the animal took shape on paper. "Know what a zebra is, Annie-kins?" Paige asked.

The beads in her hair clacked as she shook her head.

"It's a horse with striped pajamas!"

Annie giggled. "Can I make a horse in jamas?"

Paige flipped to a clean piece of paper and handed Annie the pencil, then leaned against the fence next to Hailey.

Cautiously, Hailey said, "You know, it wasn't much more than a year ago that I remember telling Karlee that I wanted a David. She said, 'You'll get one. I'm praying for him, whoever he is.' Funny thing is, that was just a few hours after I'd met Cody." She glanced sideways at Paige. "I'm praying for your Cody, whoever he is."

Paige looked down at the ground. "I wasn't serious, you know. I'm taking a sabbatical from men. This is the first time in a long time that I haven't had a guy in my life, and I'm kind of enjoying it."

Hailey laughed. "You have three French pen-pals, at least two over-seas calls a week, and who knows how many gallery customers and guys from church after you ...you're not exactly a wallflower, girl!"

"But I'm not attached, no one's running my life but me. My time is my own, I don't have to answer to anyone..."

Paige caught the worried look on Hailey's face. "Stop that! You look like my mother. I'm fine! It's possible to be happy without a man, Hailey!"

"That's not what concerns me. It's you running your own—"

"Ice cweam!" The sketch book fell to the ground as Annie pointed to two little boys with ice cream cones.

Paige crouched down beside her. "We can have ice cream after lunch. Let's go see the rhinoceros and the elephants and then it will be lunch time."

"No! Ice cweam now!" The pencil went flying.

Hailey bent down. "Annie! Let's go see the elephants!"

"Ice cweam first!"

Annie kicked the stroller and her screams got louder. People were beginning to slow down or stop to watch. A white-haired man spoke to the woman next to him in a voice meant to be overheard. "I'd like to give that child something to cry about!"

The woman answered, "A good hard swat on the behind is what she needs."

Paige clenched her teeth and lifted Annie out of the stroller. She held her tightly and rubbed her back. Through the screams, she sang in her ear, "Hip-hip-hip-hippopota-mus. Hip-hip-hip God made all of us. . ." She sang all the verses she knew of the rhyming song until Annie stopped fighting and her sobs became sniffles. Hailey pushed the stroller as they walked away from the critical eyes.

By the time they stopped in front of the elephants, Annie had forgotten all about the ice cream and was laughing at the elephants' huge ears flapping in the heat. Paige slid her back into the stroller and sighed. Hailey patted her back. "You handled that very well," she said. "I feel sorry for the family that adopts her—dealing with that all the time would be exhausting. It makes you wonder if anyone will ever want her, doesn't it?"

Paige turned away. "Someone wants her," was all she said.

three

From the long afternoon shadow of a small cherry tree, Paige glared over the edge of a framed canvas. "I know toddlers that can sit still longer than you can!"

Hailey ran her finger under the collar of the heavy buckskin dress. "Do you have any idea how hot it is in this thing?"

Paige shook her head and tried not to smile. "Do you have any idea how hard it is to paint a moving object? Your mouth is nothing but a blur! Not that Cody would recognize it any other way, but humor me anyway and freeze for five more minutes."

Hailey wiped the dampness from her top lip. "Poor choice of words," she grumbled. "I'm anything but freezing. Anyway—why do you think God invented cameras? Couldn't you just take a Polaroid of me, and then paint it?"

Paige bent to dip her brush, then tossed her head as her hair fell over her left eye. It was a habitual gesture that she knew drove her best friend crazy, and she was rewarded with an exasperated sigh from Hailey. Paige echoed the sound. "A Polaroid! A snapshot just isn't the same. If I don't capture you live I'll miss the real essence of your charm." She gave her friend a grin.

"I'm going to capture you live if—" Hailey's words were interrupted by the insistent beeping of the pager clipped to the fringe at her side. But as she reached for it, Paige yelled, "Don't move!"

"I have to look at it!"

"One minute."

"Can't I at least turn it off?"

"One minute."

"It might be an emergency."

"It's probably just your co-dependent fiancé." Paige's hands moved furiously.

"What if it's the Center?" Hailey protested.

"You're a nurse, not a brain surgeon. They can wait sixty seconds. This is crucial." Paige dipped the tip of her brush in the dab of indigo on her palette. "I'm doing your left eye and it—" She jumped as the beeper in her pocket began an off-beat duet with Hailey's. Her wide brown eyes met Hailey's blue ones. Together they grabbed pagers and read the identical messages out loud.

"This is it!" Hailey sprang up and grabbed the stool she had been sitting on. As she ran across the field toward Paige's compact car, she struggled with the button loops on her back. "I have to get out of this thing first! I can't show up in my wedding gown!" She twisted desperately to reach the loops.

"You can change when we get there! Help me get this stuff in the car!" Paige laid the wet canvas on the roof of the car. With the easel and a coffee can of clean brushes under her left arm, she opened the car door and pushed the button that popped open the trunk. As she backed out of the car, the easel slipped, banging against the inside of the door and scattering brushes on the ground. She slammed the door, threw the easel in the trunk, and bent to pick up the brushes just as Hailey reached the passenger side and yelled, "Unlock the door!"

"It isn't locked! Quit being a baby!"

"If my hands weren't full of your stuff I—" Hailey tried the handle again. "It's locked. Hurry up and un—"

Paige's face rose slowly over the roof of the car like the sun creeping over the horizon. Her eyes squinted and her teeth clenched as her hand found the door handle and pulled, to no avail. Together, they bent and stared at the gold letter "P" shining in the sunlight, dangling from the keys in the ignition. "Nooo!" Paige wailed. "My camera's in there."

Hailey leaned her forehead against the back window and stared down at her shorts and blouse and sandals on the back seat. She looked down at her bare feet, then slowly up from the fringe at her ankles to the blue beads at the waist of her wedding dress. She looked around at the field of tiger lilies behind them and the quiet stretch of gravel road in front of them. A small voice beside her said, "It's only a mile and a half to the Center."

ঌ

Perspiration coursed down Hailey's sides as they half ran, half walked into the driveway of the Sparrow Center. She let out a yell as her bare foot landed on the hot blacktop. "Now will you wear my shoes?" Paige panted. Hailey summoned her best martyr voice. "No, that's okay. You go ahead and get into the air-conditioning; I'll go around on the grass. It feels better on my ripped-up feet anyway." Paige stopped, took her shoes off, and sunk to her knees, holding her shoes above her bowed head. "Please, please, Pocahontas, take my moccasins!"

Hailey took the dusty shoes, stared at them, smiled wickedly, and said, "Well, if you insist." She sent the shoes flying toward the Center's doorway, and then she followed them across the hot black surface of the parking lot with Paige close behind, gasping, giggling, and shouting empty threats.

At the door they stopped, trying to muster some measure of composure before entering. Hailey stared at her image in the window of the building she had left just two hours earlier in her uniform. Her hand flew to her head, pulling the beaded blue headband from her sweat-dampened temples. She looked at Paige who was running long, slim, gold-and-pearl-tipped fingers through her hair. "Look at you! You don't even sweat! Look at me! Cody's here— what if he sees me? I'm not supposed to wear this 'til our wedding day! I can't go in there like this!"

"Of course you can. Just smile and act normal and walk straight back to the locker room and borrow someone's clothes!" Paige raised one eyebrow and batted her lashes. "And don't you worry," she whispered as she opened the door, "I'll take care of Cody."

As they sneaked across the carpeted floor leading to the front desk, Hailey whispered, "If my keys weren't locked in your car we could have used the back door!"

"If your keys weren't locked in my car we wouldn't need the back door!"

The day receptionist glanced up, recognized them both, and smiled as she turned back to her keyboard. Then, as the picture registered in her mind, she turned back, then stood to get a better look. Hailey smiled. "Beautiful day, isn't it, Charissa? I just can't get enough of this place!"

On the wall next to the reception desk was a large cherry wood plaque covered with brass plates. On each plate was engraved the name of a person or corporation that had donated money to build the Center. Touching one of the plates had become a ritual with Paige. Even now, in spite of the excitement of the moment, she kissed her finger and touched the words: "Karl and Madeline Prentice—in loving memory of their son, Gavin."

Entering the hallway, they broke into a run, but their flight was short-lived. Just as Hailey reached the women's locker room two men rounded the corner. Cody Worth, legal representative for the Sparrow Corporation—and Hailey's soon-to-be husband—halted abruptly at the sight of her. Robert, who was Cody's adoptive father, came to a stop next to him. Cody's dark brown eyes traveled from Hailey's long tousled hair, down the dress that his mother had been married in, to the dirty bare feet beneath it, then to the guilty expression on Paige's face. Turning to his father, he rolled his eyes and said calmly, "Looks like trouble again."

Robert nodded slowly and rubbed his chin. "Looks to me like you're eloping, son." Running his hand along his jaw in a gesture that mirrored Robert's, Cody agreed. "Bet you're right, Dad."

"Always said that was the way to go—just grab your squaw and run. In this case, it looks like the squaw is about to grab you!"

"Hey, that works. Definitely the way to go. No tux, no bouquet. . .Why waste your money on—"

"Do you mind?" Hailey nailed them with her eyes. "We're in the middle of a crisis, and a little nineties' male sensitivity would be appreciated! This is it and we're supposed to be there, but we accidentally locked the keys in the car so we need to get a ride or borrow your car, but we have to hurry! We've already walked a mile and a half and wasted a lot of time and maybe we've already missed ev—"

"Excuse me, Dad. There's only one thing to do when she gets like this." Cody took a step forward.

Hailey put her hands on her hips. "So if you would kindly just hand over your keys or give us a ride or—"

Cody put one finger under her chin, lifted her face to him, and pressed his lips against hers. Pulling away, he smiled down at her, then at Paige. "Now, is there something we can do for you ladies?"

Paige let out a loud sigh and crossed her arms in front of her, trying not to return Cody's smile. "Well, for starters you can quit being patronizing and chauvinistic."

Cody looked almost genuinely offended. "That really hurts. There's no way a man can win these days! If I offer to help I'm patronizing, if I hand you the keys I'm being insensitive, if I offer to give you a ride I'm chauvinistic, if I give you advice I'm bull-headed, if I don't I'm not caring, if I—."

"Aaah!" Paige clamped her hands over her ears. "You guys aren't even married yet and you sound just like her!"

She turned to Robert. "Dr. Worth, is there a competent person with a vehicle in this building that you could spare for half an hour?"

At that moment the back door opened and a man that neither Paige or Hailey had ever seen before walked in. Cody looked at his father, winked, and said, "Uh. . .just how, exactly, would you define 'vehicle'?"

four

"This is awesome!" Paige shouted above the beat of the helicopter's blades. She held her hair out of her eyes and laughed.

"This is insane!" Hailey retorted, as the pale green scrub suit flapped around her in the pulsing wind. The fringe of the dress she had slung over her shoulder whipped the side of her face.

"I thought you were in a hurry!" Cody yelled back over the roar.

"Not this much hurry!"

Paige laughed and tugged at Hailey's arm. "This is an adventure! Think of the story we can tell our nephew someday!"

"You can tell your nephew anything you want! I'm telling my niece that she's lucky to have at least one aunt without a death wish!" Pointing at the man who was running toward them, bent over to clear the spinning blades of the helicopter, Hailey shouted, "We don't even know this guy!"

Robert put his arm around her shoulders and pulled her back toward the building. "You don't have to do this, you know. Cody can't get away for another hour, but I can take you—I don't think they'll mind if I get there a little early!"

The back door of the Sparrow Center flew open and

Charissa ran out. "Hailey! David just called! The midwife is there and Karlee's dilated to five!"

Hailey froze, then prayed, then took a deep breath and drew on every ounce of courage she could muster. Grabbing Paige's sleeve, she yelled, "Quit standing around! When my sister finally makes up her mind to do something, she moves fast!"

Cody gave a "thumbs up" sign to the pilot, and stopped Hailey with his arm. As he was about to make introductions, the man nudged him aside, pulled off his mirrored sunglasses, and held out his hand to Hailey. "Glad to finally meet you, Hailey. I promise we'll give you a smooth ride. This'll give us time to talk about why you shouldn't marry this creep!"

Hailey gave a nervous laugh and tugged again at Paige's sleeve. Cody put his arm around her and gently pulled her hand away from Paige. Turning to his friend, he said, "Brant, I'd like you to meet Paige Stern, Hailey's housemate. Paige, this is my long lost partner in crime, Brant McCourt."

Paige extended her hand, keenly aware that the smile had faded from the man's face. He took her hand, then released it quickly without any attempt at pleasantries. She felt suddenly judged. For what, she didn't know, but she wasn't about to let this stranger intimidate her. She challenged him with her eyes and couldn't help, as she did, taking in the strong lines of his tanned face, the wavy, dark-brown hair that blew over the collar of his faded blue T-shirt. He wasn't tall, about five-foot-ten, she guessed, but his broad shoulders and muscular arms gave off a sense of power. Given any degree of internal warmth, he would have been incredibly handsome. But

Paige judged a man by his eyes, and these eyes, though disarmingly blue, cut through the July heat like icicles.

Robert ran a hand through his thick silver hair and was about to wave good-bye, but suddenly he gave in to his cautious nature. "Hey, Brant, would you mind hanging around over there. . .just in case?"

By the time Paige reached the helicopter, Hailey was in the front seat with Cody buckling her seat belt for her and talking softly to her as if she were a child. Hailey, her hands covering her face, was repeating every "fear not" Bible verse she knew out loud. Cody smiled and shook his head as Brant got in. "It's just the going up and coming down that bothers her," he yelled.

Brant laughed. "I'll stay as low to the ground as I can!" Leaning forward, Paige put her hand on Hailey's shoulder as they ascended. Considering the number of transAtlantic flights Paige had made in her life, it was hard to empathize with Hailey's phobia. But whenever the subject came up, Hailey, the nurse, had only to gently remind her that, though Paige might be able to fly over an ocean, she couldn't remove a sliver or put on a Band-Aid without passing out.

Paige heard only bits and pieces of the one-sided conversation taking place in front of her, but what she did hear only confirmed her conviction that Brant McCourt was a man who was stuck on himself. "I graduated. . .I flew. . .Canada. . .I was. . .rescue. . .then I. . ." Paige gave up counting the number of times he used the first person pronoun and shifted her attention to the bird's-eye-view of the countryside below her.

They were met at David and Karlee's back door by Karlee's best friend, Jody Hansen. "Man! You guys know how to make an entrance! Who's the hunk?"

"He's Cody's best man," Hailey answered. "How's Karlee?"

Before Jody could answer, Karlee's seven-year-old daughter Shelly came running in on tip-toes, followed shortly by a cat, two dogs, and T.J., her ten-year-old brother. T.J. let himself be hugged by Paige, while Shelly grabbed her aunts' hands. "You're supposed to go upstairs," she whispered.

Jody laughed. "Karlee's doing great; still up and walking around. The contractions are about three minutes apart."

"How's my brother holding up?" Paige asked.

"I think he's okay. He's so sweet with her!"

As she was being dragged toward the stairs, Hailey suddenly turned back and smiled at Jody. "Oh, by the way, you get to entertain 'the hunk'!"

At Jody's raised eyebrows, Paige said, "Don't worry, he'll do all the talking!"

Karlee was sitting in a carved wooden rocking chair, wearing an ivory gown, her red-gold hair pulled up in a pony tail. She didn't look up when they walked in, but continued to stare at her focal point, a quilted wall hanging draped over the end of the four-poster bed. Her fingertips moved in slow, rhythmic circles on her abdomen, in the gentle massage of effleurage. She breathed in harmony to the movement of her hands, and the only sounds in the room were the ticking of a gold clock in a bell jar on David's armoire and the soft "he-he-he" of Karlee's breathing.

Paige smiled at David, sitting on a low stool next to the rocking chair, his hand softly stroking Karlee's arm.

Behind them, through French doors, was a scene from one of the squares in the wall hanging. Sunlight shimmered on a ribbon of blue that flowed through a grove of dwarf pines. On the opposite side of the creek stood a sugar maple, full and round and green. Instinctively, Paige reached for the camera that should have been around her neck. Looking around, she spotted David's sitting on the night stand and tip-toed across the room to pick it up. She kneeled, focused, then looked up at David with a silent question. When he nodded, she pressed down on the button, capturing the moment. Karlee didn't flinch, so intense was her concentration.

Finally, after another ten seconds, she released a deep cleansing breath and raised her hand to welcome them. As Hailey walked toward her sister, she smiled at the midwife, a thin woman with straight, salt-and-pepper hair wearing a sweatshirt and faded jeans. "Hi, Diane. How's my niece doing?"

Diane leaned back against one of the bed posts and laughed, shaking her head. "Your niece has a good, strong, heart rate of 130."

"Hm. Sounds kind of nephew-ish, huh?"

"Yup. I've been wrong before—but not too often."

Bending down, Hailey kissed Karlee's cheek, then kneeled beside her, putting her face just inches from Karlee's belly. "We have to talk, baby," she whispered. "You see, if you come out with blue booties on, I have to do dishes for a whole month! Pay attention, baby, this is Aunt Hailey talking, the one who buys you presents and—"

David patted the top of her head. "Hang it up, Aunt Hailey. There isn't much he can do about it now!"

Hailey wrinkled her nose at David. "It's not fair! I put my order in long before Paige did!"

Another flash lit the room as Paige said, "Face it, Hailey, they've always liked me best."

"Yeah, well, at least I—" She felt the muscles beneath her hand tighten. "Cleansing breath," she whispered, pulling her hand away and slipping it beneath Karlee's elbow. "Good girl, nice and relaxed. Just go with it, just let your body do what it wants to do." She rubbed Karlee's arm while David did the same on the other side until the contraction ebbed.

"You were saying?" David prodded.

Hailey stared blankly at him. "Huh?"

"You said, 'Yeah, well, at least I. . .' 'At least I' what? I love to hear you two argue. It's better than anything on T.V."

"You just get vicarious pleasure out of hearing me win! I bet you never won a single fight with her when you were little!"

Paige laughed. "I never fought with David."

"That's true. I always gave in to those big brown eyes! Now she and our brother Phil were another story. . ."

"Do you have any more film?" Paige asked innocently.

"Are you changing the subject?" he answered.

"Yes, but do you have more film?"

"Top dresser drawer."

As Paige opened the drawer, she said, "So what was this 'At least I. . .' stuff, Hailey dear?"

"Oh nothing. It was too. . ." She felt a hand on her arm.

"Remember me, guys?" Karlee said, then shifted her eyes to the wall hanging and blew out a forceful breath. When the contraction was over, Karlee held her arm out to

David. "Help me up," she said. Slowly, she waddled over to a window. "I'm not crazy after all!" she cried. "There really is a helicopter in my back yard. What on earth?"

Hailey laughed. "Don't ask. It's a long story. It all started with Paige locking her keys—and my clothes—in the car and—"

"It did not!" Paige protested. "It all started with Hailey dragging me out to this field of tiger lilies to. . .never mind."

David put one hand to his forehead, while the other gently rubbed Karlee's back as she leaned against him. "Could we go back to the 'at least I' thing? That promised to be very entertaining."

Her face pressed against David's chest, Karlee's voice was lost to the others as she asked, "What about the helicopter?"

"Yeah, let's go back to the 'at least I' thing," Paige taunted. "You were about to say. . .?"

"What about the heli. . ." Karlee asked quietly between pants.

"Never mind, it was too nasty. Even I can be sensitive at times, Paige dear."

"What. . .about. . .the. . ."

"Oh, no, you're not going to get out of it that easily! You had something deliciously rude planned for me and it's only fair that I get a chance at a comeback!"

"What. . .about. . ."

"I'll save it for a time when I really need it. The birth of our niece is a time of happiness and joy and I will not shatter the wonder of this day with—"

"WHAT ABOUT THE STUPID HELICOPTER?!?"

five

When the shock wave finally subsided, Diane smiled at the stunned faces, none more surprised at the outburst than Karlee herself. "I believe," Diane said, "that we have reached the stage of labor known as transition."

Karlee leaned heavily against David and began her breathing again, her pace faster than before. One hand went to her back as the contraction peaked and Hailey noted a momentary loss of concentration as the intensity surprised her. Karlee's other hand gripped David's shoulder and she squeezed her eyes shut. Hailey moved quietly behind them and pressed the heel of her hand firmly but gently against Karlee's lower back as David whispered against her hair. "Just relax, honey, I've got you." He put his hand over hers until he felt her grip loosen beneath his touch.

When the contraction was over, Karlee said, "I think I'll get in bed now."

Hailey smiled at her, recognizing the universal look of a woman in labor, a look that announced she was entering her own private world, focused solely on the work at hand. As Diane readied pillows and helped Karlee find a comfortable position, Hailey drew the room-darkening blinds and crossed the room to turn on a small lamp.

Paige put her hand on David's shoulder. "I'll go get some coffee," she said. Several seconds passed before her words registered with David. When he finally looked up at her, her heart wrenched at the look on his face. Memories, like specters from a never-forgotten nightmare, hovered around him and were mirrored in his eyes. This was how he had lost his first wife, and tears stung Paige's eyes as she wrapped her arms around her brother. "It's gonna be okay this time," she whispered.

His arms tightened around her. "Can we pray before you go?"

Paige stood next to Diane, her hand resting on the sheet covering Karlee's leg. Across the bed, David held Karlee's hand and Hailey stood next to him, her head bowed. Their silence lasted through two contractions. Then, rubbing his thumb across the back of Karlee's hand, David began to pray.

"Thank You, Lord. I don't have words to express how grateful I am for this child and for the family you have given me. Thank You for letting us share this joy at home. Thank You for Diane, for her skill and compassion. . ." He smiled across the bed at the midwife. "And for her patience with me over the past nine months. Thank You for Paige and Hailey, for their constant support and their ability to make us laugh when we need it. Father, You know our past losses and our fears. Help us to leave them with You and remember Your promises." He stopped for a minute, locking eyes with his wife of one year. "Help me to be strong for Karlee, Lord, and help me be a good father."

Karlee squeezed his hand. Before another contraction began, she had time to whisper, "You already are."

Paige pulled tissues from the box on the night stand, kept one for herself, and handed one to Hailey. The understanding in Paige's eyes spoke volumes and Hailey smiled through her tears and hugged her. "What would I do without you?"

"Probably lead a peaceful life," Paige responded. "I'll bring you some coffee."

David nodded toward the window just as Paige was about to step out of the room. "Brant's still here?" he asked.

Paige nodded. "Robert asked him to stay."

David smiled sympathetically. "That must be awkward for you."

Giving him a confused look, Paige shrugged. "He is a bit egotistical, isn't he? But he's Jody's problem right now, I guess." She turned then, missing the questioning look on her brother's face.

At one end of the high-ceilinged great room, T.J. and Shelly were sitting on the floor playing a board game. Just two feet away, Brant half-sprawled on the couch, one leg over the arm, the other foot on the deep-piled rug. He was peering over Shelly's shoulder, giving her advice on her next move.

T.J. was the first to see Paige descending the stairs. His tattling was not totally serious, but the look on his face was a good attempt. "Aunt Paige, tell him to quit giving Shelly answers! They're cheating!"

At the mention of Paige's name, Brant sat upright. Even though Paige's first impression had not been favorable, the prayer time upstairs had put her in a softer mood, and she was willing to give him a second chance. "Who's winning?" she asked.

A robin could have landed on Shelly's pouting lip. "He is," she whined, squinting at her brother.

Paige winked at T.J. "They're cheating and you're still winning? I wouldn't worry about it, Teej." Then she turned to Brant, who was nervously turning his watch back and forth on his arm. "I'm getting some coffee for the people upstairs. Would you like some?"

"Thank you, but Jody is keeping me supplied."

Paige nodded and walked to the other end of the great room where Jody was just walking out of the pantry, her arms laden with bread, corn chips, and a jar of apple sauce. She jumped as Paige reached out to grab the jar from her. "Sorry, just trying to help," Paige laughed.

"Thanks. I'm jumpy, I guess. It's hard being down here and wondering what's going on upstairs."

"She's in transition. Why don't you go on up for a while?"

Jody laughed. "No thanks. As I recall that's the stage of labor where you start throwing whatever you can get your hands on and telling your husband you're putting him on the next plane to Siberia!"

"Jody! You didn't do that to poor Don, did you?"

Setting the bread down on the counter, Jody gave a deep throated laugh. "Why do you think we stopped at two kids?"

Paige shook her head and took two mugs out of the cupboard. Lowering her voice, she said, "So how are you and the fly guy getting along?"

"Fine! Makes me wish I was young and single!" Jody whispered. "Like you, for instance."

"You don't find him a bit grating?"

Jody's brow furrowed. "Not at all! He's fascinating. I take it you don't agree?"

"I don't know. . ." Paige poured coffee from the coffee

maker into an insulated pot as she thought about her answer. "There's something cold about him. Maybe it's just the 'been there, done that' attitude."

"I don't see it as bragging—he really has been there and done that! He's had the kids spellbound with his stories since he got here!"

"What kind of stories?"

"Oh, things like finding himself face to face with a grizzly while he was rescuing some lost elk hunters in Canada, and being stuck in a cabin for two weeks with snow up to the roof. . ."

"And you believe all that?"

"Paige! You're so cynical! Just look into those beautiful blue eyes and you'll know he's not capable of lying! He's really sweet—you just got a wrong first impression. Do you know anything about him?"

"No. I've heard Cody talk about him, but I never paid much attention."

"He just moved back here from Canada. He was on a search and rescue team up there. Now he's working part-time as a paramedic for the city and part-time as a Flight-for-Life pilot and he's trying to start his own medical transport company. He inherited a piece of land out on Old Miller Road and he's had it re-zoned and he's planning to start building in the fall. The closest private transport company is in Madison, so our EMTs and rescue equipment get tied up with non-emergency calls. There's a real need for what he's doing."

"And he's going to hire you for PR, right?"

"He wouldn't have to twist my arm too far! I'm telling you, girl, give him a second chance."

Paige rolled her eyes and set the coffee pot on a tray

with four cups. Jody threw up her hands in a gesture of exasperation and said, "I'm going to make sandwiches for you guys and set them in the hallway upstairs. If Karlee's anything like I was, she won't be able to stand the smell of food right now."

Paige laughed, picked up the tray, walked three steps, and turned. "Siberia, huh?"

Stopping next to the couch she asked, "Those two still cheating, T.J.?"

"Yeah. But I don't care. I'm still ahead."

Paige laughed and had started turning toward the stairs when Brant McCourt got to his feet. "Can I. . .carry that for you?"

Trying to read the look in his eyes, Paige stared at him for a moment before answering. The arrogance was still evident in the slight tip of his chin, but it was combined with something that made her even more uncomfortable. She could only define it as sheer embarrassment, as if the very act of offering to help a woman was degrading. She tightened her grip on the tray. "No. . .I've got it."

Brant rubbed his hand over the dark shadow on his chin. "Listen, this isn't a good time, but—"

The back door opened and Robert Worth stepped in. He greeted Jody, then crossed the floor to Paige and Brant. "How's it going?"

"Getting close, I guess. Karlee didn't seem to be in the mood for any more pictures at the moment so I thought I'd do a coffee run."

Robert laughed. "Yeah, David said you were a wimp."

"Hey, we all have our gifts here! Hailey's the coach, Jody's the baby-sitter, and I'm photographer and gopher!"

"In other words, you're the one who gets to run when

you can't handle it!"

"Exactly!"

"So, after all those reasons they gave for choosing home birth, it was really just that they didn't want you creating a scene at the hospital!"

Paige laughed and stepped toward the stairs. "Doctors give me hives!"

Robert laughed, then turned serious. "How's David?"

"He's doing all right. We spent some time in prayer. That helped."

"Good." Robert nodded, then turned to Brant, whose gaze was following Paige up the stairs. "Thanks for staying. I'm sure everything is going to go fine, but I've always been the overly-cautious type."

They sat down on the couch and Robert talked to T.J. and Shelly for several minutes, and then to Brant. "Has Cody given you any history on this wonderfully strange family he's marrying into?"

As Brant answered, "A little," Shelly smiled and wrinkled her nose at Robert.

"Well, let me fill you in on what you might have missed," Robert began. "David and his wife Shawna built this house, then they were called to Senegal as missionaries. They were there for three years and Shawna died in childbirth. Matthew, the baby, only lived for about an hour. David moved back here and the Lord gave him a vision for the Sparrow Center. It was the only thing that kept him going for awhile. "Before the Center was built he met the mother of these adorable kids." This time, both Shelly and T.J. smiled. "They lost their father in a construction accident two years ago. Karlee and David were married last summer. Now Hailey, Karlee's sister, and Paige, who, in case no one's told you, is David's sister, are now living in Karlee's house." Robert looked at the kids. "Did I miss anything?"

Shelly wrinkled her nose again, "You have to say, 'and they had a baby and lived happily ever after. The end.'"

❧

Her timing was perfect. When Paige slipped back into the bedroom, she had just enough time to set down the tray and pick up the camera before a loud, clear, incredible cry broke the silence in the room.

"It's a boy!" Diane announced over the wail. "A beautiful, healthy, baby boy!"

Paige watched in awe as the purplish bundle Diane held quickly turned pink and continued to cry until he was placed in his mother's arms. Instinctively knowing that he was where he belonged, Jordan Matthew Stern whimpered twice and nestled against his mother's breast.

six

Hailey leaned against the railing of the balcony outside David and Karlee's bedroom. She closed her eyes, letting the balmy night breeze soothe her. When she heard the French doors open, she didn't turn around; she knew who it was. Tilting her head back, she stared up at the star-spattered sky and sighed as Cody's arms wrapped around her waist. Softly in her right ear she heard the words only he knew she so desperately needed to hear at that moment.

"I can hardly wait to see our child in your arms some-day," he whispered. Two and a half years had passed since her abortion, yet the pain still came in waves, fol-lowed always by another small step in her healing jour-ney. This day had been a roller-coaster of emotions in spite of the thought and prayer she'd put into preparing for it. She'd been strong for David and Karlee, slipping easily into her role as nurse and coach. She hadn't needed to pretend to be elated when Jordan Matthew came into the world. It was only in the quiet hours since then that grief and regrets had found unguarded moments to steal back in.

Cody turned her slowly to face him and his arms tight-ened around her, giving her permission to cry once again. When her tears were spent, she pulled Cody's face down to hers and kissed him. "I love you," she whispered.

"I know," he said. Picking up the two glasses of iced

tea he had brought out with him, he handed one to her. "Take a sip." She did, and he searched her eyes, reading her mood. "You okay, Little Foot?"

Hailey nodded. "I'm okay."

"You need to get home to bed."

She shrugged. "I'm off tomorrow; I can sleep in." She tried to stifle a yawn. "It's been a crazy day."

"It's been a crazy year." Cody laughed at the look on her face. "Nice crazy," he added hastily. Putting his lips close to her ear, he whispered impatiently, "Twenty-four days!"

Hailey gently pulled free and turned, staring up at the stars, so he couldn't see her face. "You know, I've been thinking. . .with the baby coming so late, this only gives Karlee three weeks to recover. What if she's not up to it? Her dress might not fit right and she might not have her strength back. Is it really wise to take a three-week-old to a wedding with all those people and all those germs? I've decided we need to postpone it a good month or two. In fact, I think a Christmas wed—" The hand that clamped over her mouth muffled her words but didn't stop them.

Cody's eyes shone with mischief. "Look woman, let's get this perfectly clear. Twenty-four days from today, at three o'clock in the afternoon, I am standing on the river-bank and pledging my life to someone, and then dragging that someone off to a romantic cabin in Montana for two weeks. Now, if you're not interested in being that some-one, I'm sure I can ask P—" Hailey's lips landed squarely on his and she somehow managed to kiss him while laughing at the same time.

"Paige is right!" she said as she pulled away. "You're starting to sound just like me!"

"Scary thought!" Cody said under his breath as he turned her toward the door. "Really scary thought!"

❧

Diane had given orders before she left for David to clear out the visitors and let Karlee sleep. While she slept, Jody kept everyone downstairs fed and entertained. When they were allowed back upstairs, Karlee was wearing a pink gown with a matching hair band. Her legs were drawn up and the baby's head rested against her knees, his tiny feet against her chest. She stroked the fuzzy, inch-long hair that was the color of blackened copper. Paige flashed the camera incessantly as she picked her way across the room, maneuvering around pets and people to capture every move the baby made and the reactions on the faces of his audience. Hailey rolled her eyes as Paige aimed the lens at her, catching her with her head against Cody's arm. Paige smiled and winked. "A good one!" she whispered.

Hours past his bedtime, T.J. was still bouncing off the walls, telling anyone who cared to listen, "I knew it was going to be a boy! I told all of you it was going to be a boy and I was right!" Shelly, who was wound up in her own quiet way, cooed and giggled and couldn't keep her hands off the baby's downy head. But of all the day's picture-memories that would stay in Paige's mind, the look of awe on David's face would always be most precious. When Karlee laid the baby, just minutes old, in David's arms and whispered, "Here's your son," there had not been a dry eye in the room.

❧

The hot mid-morning sun streamed in the open window. Hailey lay buried beneath the sheet with only her left foot exposed. She sat up slowly, then slumped back against her four pillows, yawned and stretched and smiled smugly. It was her first day off in twelve days and she intended to savor the freedom. She opened one eye and glanced at the digital clock: 10:06 A.M. She rose slowly and stretched again. Still sitting on the edge of the bed, she slipped her feet into her teddy bear slippers. She had only one plan for the day—to do nothing that was not convenient. With that in mind, she pondered the immediate options: should she take a shower, call Cody, eat breakfast, call Cody, call David and Karlee, eat lunch, call Cody, or fall back onto the covers?

As she weighed the possibilities, Karlee's eleven-year-old calico cat, Mrs. Patches, slunk into the room, winding her body against the door frame. Hailey had brought her home with her the night before since the feline's curiosity over the new arrival was bothering Karlee. Hailey reached down near the floor and let Mrs. Patches rub her graying face against her arm, then ran her hand along her soft side. "Morning, you old—eeoo!"

Hailey stared at the sticky swirls of green and blue paint on the cat's fur and the matching streaks on her hand. "This better not be from my picture!" She flew down the stairs, checking the easels in the living room and dining room for signs of damage as she ran, and stopped at the door of what had once been Karlee's den. The table and floor were littered with half-painted canvases, paintbrushes, cloths, and easels.

With relief, she realized that her portrait was still in the trunk of Paige's car which Cody and Brant had rescued sometime during yesterday's confusion. Spotting the altered landscape painting leaning against the wall, Hailey laughed and spoke to the cat. "You're a natural,

Mrs. Picasso! Looks like the first hurricane to hit central Wisconsin!" Grabbing a can of paint thinner, she back-tracked into the kitchen and listened to the phone messages while she started the coffee pot, then headed for the bathroom, coaxing Mrs. Patches to follow.

Fifteen minutes later, when she walked out of the bathroom with a clean cat at her feet, Paige was walking in the back door, wearing heels and a black suit with a purple satin blouse, and a large leather portfolio under her arm. "Mmm coffee!" she said.

Without a word, Hailey thrust the can of paint thinner into her hand. "Mmm turpentine!" she said. "The cat has been making improvements on some of your work." Over Paige's wail, Hailey yelled, "You two work well together!"

When the last trace of paint had been removed from door frames and chair legs, they finally sat down for their first cup of coffee. Paige, now in tan shorts and red shirt, was just beginning to see the humor in the situation. "I was getting so many interruptions at the gallery; I thought I'd come home and sit on the porch and work in the peace and quiet of my own home!"

Hailey laughed. "Why don't you get settled out on the porch and I'll make some omelets." At the look of horror on Paige's face, she said, "Better I practice on you than Cody."

Picking up her portfolio, Paige muttered, "I guess I can be sacrificed for the cause."

Half an hour later, after donating her first attempt to the compost pile, Hailey handed Paige a plate. To sidetrack any remarks about her cooking, she quickly asked Paige, "Did you get your messages off the answering machine?"

"No, I got a late start this morning. Who called?"

Hailey sat down on a chintz-cushioned wicker chair. Tapping her head, she said, "I'm not sure my computer has that much memory. Let's see. . .Stuart from Sunday School wants to know if you'll go on the church hay ride with him. . .which is only about nine weeks away! Nothing like planning ahead. Then there was Peter calling from Paris again, and. . .who in the world is Pablo?"

Paige stuffed a huge bite of egg in her mouth to avoid answering. Hailey, tired of waiting for an answer, decided to take advantage of the silence. "Karlee said you were asking about buying the house. You gonna marry Pablo the mystery man and settle down here?" When all she got was an irritated sigh, she asked seriously, "What are you waiting for?"

There was no sense pretending she didn't understand the question. Paige shrugged. "Not Pablo!" She squirmed under her best friend's gaze, then suddenly remembered some old business. "That's what that nasty little remark was about, right? 'At least I'. . .At least I got the guy, right? At least I got Cody, at least I'm getting married?"

Hailey's brow furrowed at the defensiveness in Paige's voice. "It was a joke, girl! You've got guys coming out of the woodwork after you!"

"Marriage isn't for everyone! Who says I have to be Mrs. Somebody to be happy? I don't need to be washing some guy's smelly socks and sharing his checkbook to be fulfilled!"

Hailey leaned forward, wanting to laugh, yet held in check by the passion on Paige's face. "When you put it like that, neither do I! You make marriage sound like a life sentence on the chain gang! Who have you been listening to? It's not like that, Paige! I may gain a new title as

Cody's wife, but I don't lose me! I'm deeper, stronger because of him, not weaker!" Her voice softened, sensing her friend's turmoil. "I watched you holding the baby last night. That was not the face of a woman willing to give up her dreams of motherhood!"

Staring out the window at the swing set in the backyard, Paige quietly said, "We were talking about marriage, not motherhood."

They ate in silence for several minutes. Paige set her plate on the floor and picked up her laptop computer. Hailey stood, picked up the plates, and stared at her friend wondering what was behind the recent turmoil of emotions. A thought crossed her mind and she asked softly, "Ever wonder what your life would have been like if Gavin Prentice were still alive?"

Paige looked up, stared out the window again, and smiled wistfully. "Every day. I'd probably be on a cruise right now. . ."

Sitting back down on the arm of the chair, Hailey said, "You never talk about him."

Shrugging her shoulders, Paige said, "Gavin is like a dream, like something that never really happened. It was right after Shawna died and Mom and I flew out here to help David get settled. David was so depressed. . .one day I just had to get away, so I went into town and had lunch all by myself. Until this gorgeous stranger walked up and introduced himself!" Paige sighed. "I probably saw him for a total of eight hours—two dates—and then I went back to college."

"But then there were the letters. . ." Hailey coaxed.

Paige sighed. "And then the letters. Gavin was smooth in person, almost too smooth, you know? He looked like a tennis player in a *GQ* ad—tall, sandy blond hair, green eyes like you've never seen before. You know. . .the rich, handsome, candy and flowers type; the kind you're attracted to, but don't know if you should trust?"

Hailey laughed. "Believe me, I know!"

"I was sure that the minute I left here, probably before I landed back in Connecticut, he'd be out with someone else. But I wrote to him anyway, just to see what would happen. I was amazed that he wrote back and amazed at his letters. They were so sincere. . .not smooth, just sincere." Paige looked down, sliding her pearl ring back and forth on her finger. "It was like on paper he could forget that his father was a millionaire and that he was being groomed to follow in his footsteps. He could be real and talk about the things that really mattered. We even wrote poems for each other. It was never romantic, but I could tell him anything. It was almost like writing a journal. I sometimes wish I had the courage to ask his family if they ever found my letters. It would give me insight into who I was then. Sometimes I feel. . .I don't know. I guess I miss who I used to be."

Hailey nodded, encouraging Paige to go on.

"He never wrote about what he was doing, the day to day things, it was always deep—questions about God and the meaning of life." Paige turned away from the window and looked up at Hailey. "He seemed so close to accepting Christ. The day before his plane crashed he wrote a poem for me that was almost a prayer. . .but I'll never know for sure if he gave his life to Christ or not—at least not this side of heaven, anyway."

"Can I ask you something?" Hailey asked. When Paige nodded, she said, "Do you think you're comparing every guy you meet with Gavin?"

Paige smiled. "I know I am, and maybe it's not fair, but I'd rather not have a relationship at all if it can't be that open. I want what you've got, but every guy I meet wants to own me or change me! Why should I settle for something less than what I know is possible?"

seven

Cody glanced again at his watch. Another ten minutes
had passed. He lifted a chain saw from the back of
Brant's 1946 midnight-blue pickup, then set it down
again. He couldn't do a thing until Brant showed up to
tell him where to start, and his patience was wearing thin.
He'd promised half of his day to Brant to help him clear
trees from a parcel of the land he'd just inherited. The
other half of the day belonged to Hailey, and there was no
way that Brant's time was going to overlap hers! It wasn't
like Brant to be late. But then, the presence of the truck
next to the old deserted logging road proved that he'd
actually been there before Cody. And it was like Brant to
get distracted.

Cody walked to the edge of the trees and called his
name for the tenth time, but his only answer came from
the red squirrel on a limb above him. He walked back and
circled the truck again, admiring the workmanship. It was
hard to believe this was the same piece of machinery
Brant had uncovered six years ago in his grandfather's
barn. He'd found it sitting on blocks, the axles gone, the
body weather-worn though not badly rusted, and only one
window intact. The upholstery had been home to several
generations of mice. But what stood before him now
looked like a showroom model and ran as smooth as it
looked.

Helping himself to the contents of the cooler in the back of the pickup, Cody dug through the mound of ice and pulled out a can of root beer. Easing his long frame to the ground, he rested the back of his head on the running board and drained the can. Then, slamming it between his hands, he lay down on the uncut grass and closed his eyes, relaxing in the growing warmth of the morning light.

As the sun rose higher in the sky, Cody stirred at the sound of a motorcycle approaching, a strange sound on the little-used road that divided the property once owned by Brant's grandfather. To his knowledge, Brant owned nothing smaller than the truck, but nothing about this old friend would surprise him. Fighting his curiosity, he lay still, pretending to be oblivious to the roaring of the ancient engine in desperate need of a new muffler. It had to be Brant.

When the noise and the vehicle finally came to a stop, the narrow, bald front wheel was only six inches from Cody's head. The familiar laugh above him was reward enough for not flinching.

"Red man has nerves of steel. I could have left tread marks on that pretty face, you know."

Cody rolled over slowly, poked his finger at a bulging spot on the tire, and laughed. "Says white man who cries over road kill!"

"Shhh. . .I got a rep to protect!" Brant extended his hand and Cody rose to his feet, shaking off the dust and fine gravel that Brant's approach had coated him with.

"Don't worry, your secret's safe with me—unless I need to use it, of course!"

Brant laughed and shook his head. "As would any self-respecting lawyer! Hey, you know the difference between a catfish and a lawyer?"

Cody rolled his eyes, amazed that there was a lawyer joke he hadn't heard yet.

"One's a scum-sucking bottom dweller. The other one's a fish!"

Cody sighed, threw the crumpled can at Brant, and pointed his foot at the motorcycle. "So what's this hunk of junk and where have you been?"

Brant pulled a blue bandanna from his pocket and used it to wipe the dust and sweat from his face. "Found this in the chicken coop. I did some work on it and thought I'd bring it out here to try it out. Got just over the hill and she stalled, then I flooded her, so I had to wait it out. Sorry." He caressed the handlebars as he talked. "1957 Harley. It'll take some elbow grease. . ."

"And an arm and a leg," Cody added.

"Yeah, but picture this baby when I'm done. Maroon metal-flake with a gold gas tank. . .she'll be sweet! I could sell her for five digits!"

"Like you'd ever part with one of your toys!"

"I may have to if my business loan doesn't go through. I can't start a business on what I make from selling fire-wood."

"Are you worried about it? You're a land owner now, you've got collateral."

"Yeah, but I can't even pay taxes on the place if I don't start making some decent money soon! I've spent most of my inheritance on a helicopter that has shrapnel scars from Vietnam and a Cessna that was born before I was!"

"I guess you are a risk, come to think of it!"

Brant picked up a chain saw and handed it to Cody, then reached for the other saw and the gas can. Cody grabbed the cooler and, as they began walking toward the woods, said, "So tell me, in view of your fascination with dilapidated things, how old do you like your women?"

Smiling, Brant answered, "If I could find a woman as good looking and dependable as my truck I wouldn't care how old she was!"

"Good looking and dependable, huh? Any other qualifications?"

"This is not a hypothetical question, is it?"

"Very astute. There is someone I had in mind."

"She's not my type."

"I haven't mentioned any names yet."

Brant laughed. "You were anything but subtle yesterday when you suggested I teach her to fly in exchange for painting lessons. Like I've always wanted to do water color! I fully expected you to propose for me right on the spot!"

"Hey, I was just taking my cues from Jody! Now there's a woman who missed her calling!"

"Yeah, Yenta the matchmaker!"

"I was thinking she'd make a great talk show host!" Cody set the cooler down and held an imaginary microphone at arm's length. "Paige, dear, tell this nice, handsome, single man what a wonderfully warm, talented, and articulate, not to mention single, woman you are!" Picking up the cooler again, he said, "Seriously, I think you and Paige are perfect for each other!"

Brant took a deep breath and looked away. Almost to himself he said, "I wish." Then, with an intensity that surprised Cody, he said, "Look at her! She's rich, spoiled, artsy. . .she had gold fingernails with little pearls glued to them, for heaven's sakes! And the way she kept tossing her hair. . .made me want to chop it off!"

Cody, who hadn't noticed the color of Paige's finger-nails, even though he'd been around her for hours the night before, turned away and smiled to himself. "So what are you looking for? Besides reliable and dependable."

"Someone earthy, adventurous."

"She wants to learn to fly a plane! How much more adventurous can you get?"

Brant took out a spray can and marked a blaze-orange X on the tree in front of him, then moved on. "You don't think for a minute she was serious, do you? Pretending to be interested in a guy's hobbies is the oldest trick in the book!"

"So you're saying she was just coming on to you? You think she's interested?"

Brant flexed his right arm. "How could she not be?"

Cody rolled his eyes, but Brant only shrugged his shoulders. "Well? Women like me, what can I say? But for once I'd like to find a girl who's not stuck on herself, someone who doesn't go through withdrawal symptoms if she's away from a mirror for an hour! I want a woman who's low maintenance, you know? Who cares more about inner beauty than peach satin and pearls!"

After several seconds, Cody managed to recall that Paige had been wearing a satin blouse yesterday. Had he been quizzed, he would have guessed it was pink, but obviously Brant had paid closer attention to details. With exaggerated compassion in his voice he quoted, "'Who can find a virtuous woman? For her price is far above rubies!'"

Not responding to the sarcasm, Brant marked another tree and kept talking. "And I want a family. Just being there yesterday when the baby was born. . .I've done a dozen emergency deliveries, but they never got to me like this one. Hearing that first cry, even from downstairs. . . and seeing the looks on those kids' faces, and David and Karlee together. . .I want that."

Cody stared at his friend as if seeing him for the first time. This sudden bout of seriousness was so out of character it was all he could do not to laugh. Brant unscrewed the gas cap on his chain saw and looked inside. Replacing the cap, he stood still for a minute, then looked beyond Cody, deep into the trees.

"My tastes have changed so much in the past five years. All those years you were talking to me about God and telling me how great it was to be a Christian, you never prepared me for that! That not only would my life change, but I'd change. Who would have thought I'd be looking for a woman who loves kids! I'm plenty ready to settle down, but it's got to be with someone challenging, with real depth, someone who's really passionate about serving God! Are there women like that really out there?"

Finally letting himself smile, Cody said, "Sorry pal, I got the last one." They walked in silence, Brant marked two more trees, and then Cody said, "Don't be too quick to rule out Paige. There's more to her than satin and pearls."

Shaking his head, Brant said, "Hang it up, Code, even if I could get beyond the fingernails and the hair thing, she's got an attitude I can't tolerate."

"What do you mean?"

"I don't know. . .isn't she supposed to be a Christian? But instead all she seems interested in is. . .oh, you know, Paris and the 'Gallery'. . .been there, done that, you know? There's no way that you're hooking me up with Cleopatra!"

Cody turned slowly and stared at Brant. "You just met her yesterday and she told you about that?"

Brant's face blazed red. "Well, I. . .I guess someone mentioned it. . ."

"No way! No one in that house 'just happened to mention' the time Paige was performing as Cleopatra and ended up falling off the stage in a gold lamé dress! When David told Hailey and me about it, we laughed for three hours and Paige didn't talk to any of us for a week! She made us sign an oath in blood not to repeat it! Where did you hear about that?"

"I, uh, well—"

Brant's excuses were drowned in the roar of the chain saw.

eight

Taking a calming breath, Paige settled herself on a cushion on the floor and began arranging brushes and tubes of paint in front of her. Painting, especially the kind she did here at the Center, was usually relaxing. The whimsical style had always come naturally to her. Before she had been offered a scholarship to study "serious" art in Paris, all she had wanted to do was illustrate children's books. Now she painted landscapes and portraits and collected books illustrated by other artists while her sketch books collected dust in the closet.

She looked up and down the hallway, picturing the finished job. This was her last project until the new wing of the Sparrow Center was finished. She'd spent most of the previous summer covering the walls of the lobby and day room with jungle-theme murals. Then, after returning from Europe in the spring, she had started in on smaller scenes in the resident rooms.

She'd planned to finish weeks earlier, but volunteering to help the occupational therapy team had cut into her time. It had also introduced her to Annie. She looked at the crayon drawing sitting next to her on the floor and sighed. She hadn't planned on painting tonight and the mood she was in wasn't conducive to creativity. What she had planned on was supper with Annie and then curling up together with a stack of Winnie the Pooh books. Instead, she'd spent an extra hour on the freeway when a gruesome accident had backed up traffic for almost an hour and her car had overheated. On top of that, she hadn't thought to check Annie's schedule, and as it turned out, she'd had five minutes with her before a group of volunteer "Grammas" had come to take her and several other residents out for dinner.

Sliding the drawing into her canvas bag on top of the books she'd brought, she pulled out her CD player, hoping a few minutes with Michael Card would soothe her spirits. Adjusting her headphones, she pushed "play," picked up her pencil, closed her eyes, and tried to envision a zebra leaping through a field of tall grass. What she saw instead was the underside of the Flight-for-Life helicopter flying over her and the flashing lights of two rescue squads pulling away from the accident scene. She turned the volume knob on the CD player, and waited, but all she got was silence. Looking down, she saw the CD sitting motionless beneath the player's window. The batteries were dead.

"Rats!" She tore the headphones off and slammed them on the floor. Picking up the pillow, she threw it down the hall and watched as it skidded across the floor and into the break room. Not bothering to go after it, she walked into the store room that David, whose architectural firm had designed the Sparrow Center, was using as a temporary office. She began rifling through drawers, hunting for batteries, and making so much noise she didn't hear David come to the doorway.

"What, exactly, are you looking for?" The amusement was clear in her brother's eyes. Paige mumbled an answer and moved to the next drawer, turning her back on him.

"This is just like old times," David said, "You, in my room, rummaging through my stuff without my permission. If I had the slightest idea what you just said I might be able to help you."

Paige banged a cupboard door shut and threw up her hands. "You'd think in all this junk there'd be a couple measly little double A batteries!"

Putting his hands on her shoulders, David turned her to face him. "Take a deep breath, kid. What's the matter."

"My batteries are dead."

"It's not dead batteries that have you wound this tight." He guided her to a chair and gently pushed her into it. "Talk, woman."

"There was this horrible accident on the freeway tonight and I can't get it out of my head and all my plans for the weekend got screwed up and. . ."

"And. . .?"

"I want to have a child."

David sat down heavily on the corner of the desk. "Say, what? Are you. . .pregnant?"

"No! David! Of course not!"

"So what are you talking about?"

"Oh, David, you're so traditional, so conventional. You'll think I'm crazy."

"I've thought that before. Try me."

"A child. I want one."

"I assume you're talking about marriage first and then a baby?"

"No! I'm not talking about marriage at all! I'm not even talking about a baby!"

"You're right, I'm way too conventional. I haven't got a clue what you're talking about and you're scaring me.

This isn't like you, Paige."

"I'm going to be thirty in two years and I want to be a mother! Hailey got the last decent, marriageable guy in the United States, and besides, I'm not sure I'm the marriage-type anyway. I just want to be a mother." She looked at David's confused expression and turned away from him. "I want to adopt Annie," she said quietly.

"Whoa. . ." David stood, then dropped into the chair across from her. "Have you talked to Robert about this?"

"No. I haven't talked to anyone yet. But I know that her mother is relinquishing her rights, and there's no father in the picture."

David ran his hand over his face. As president of the Center's board, he knew things that Paige didn't, things he couldn't talk about yet. He sighed, hating to see her get hurt. "Adoption can be a complicated thing, Paige; there could be a lot of obstacles in your way. I hate to see you get your hopes up. Have you really thought about it? Do you realize what kind of commitment it would take? Annie is a precious little girl, but raising her would be a minute-by-minute challenge, maybe for the rest of your life."

"I've thought about it, David. Annie needs a real home and I need a purpose in life."

"Have you prayed about it? Keep in mind, little sister, that good will is not always God's will."

"Please. Spare me the sermon, David. I was counting on your love and support. Do I have it or don't I?"

"My love, always. My support. . .I don't know." He stood, then bent down and wrapped her in a bear hug. "But I will pray about it," he said.

Walking into the break room to get her pillow, the first

thing Paige saw was a pair of leather boots sitting next to the couch. The next thing she saw was her pillow—wedged beneath Brant's head on the couch. His eyes were closed and Paige couldn't help but sigh in exasperation at his gall. She hoped he would hear her, but not a muscle moved. Opening the refrigerator, she whispered, "Welcome to the Holiday Inn, sir."

Grabbing a can of tomato juice, she let the door slam, and turned to see if it produced a reaction. He still appeared to be sleeping like a baby. "Of all the nerve," she sighed. Pulling the tab off the juice can, she studied him, wondering why he wore wool socks in the summer, what it said on his brass belt buckle, and if he owned anything other than faded T-shirts. She let her eyes travel up to the sun-streaked hair that curled at his neck and the strong jaw.

She took a drink, then looked back at him, and almost choked. His eyes were open, wide open, and the small curves at the corners of his mouth said he was enjoying every second of her discomfort. Recovering as gracefully as she could, she said, "When you're done with your nap I'd like my pillow back."

"No problem," he said, smiling wider as he closed his eyes again.

Paige shook her head in disbelief and headed for the door. She wasn't going to start a fight. Not over a pillow, and not with the likes of Brant McCourt.

His voice stopped her in her tracks and pulled her back. "I don't think your adopting Annie is such a good idea."

"Of all the. . .I can't believe. . ." was all she managed as she stormed back into the room.

"Look," he said, "I know it's none of my business, but—"

"It's one thing to overhear a private conversation, Mr. McCourt. It's an altogether different thing to think you've got a right to get involved in it!"

Brant sat up. Mocking her formality, he said, "Miss Stern, would it be possible for you to cut me some slack? If you really want a reason to be mad at me I can give you one, but if you could just give me one minute. . ."

"Did it occur to you that I might not be interested in listening to your opinion about my future?"

"Just who *are* you listening to these days? Seems to me you don't hear much beyond your own voice."

"How dare you!"

Brant shoved one foot into a boot and said, "I dare because I've been there, Miss Stern! I think you've got your own interests in mind here and not what's best for that little girl!"

Paige gripped the back of a chair. Never in her adult life had she had such a conversation with a virtual stranger. "You've been hanging around here for one week and already you're an expert on the residents' welfare, and mine, too? What do you know about Annie, and what could you possibly know about me?"

Brant put on his other boot, picked up her pillow, and stood. She challenged his arrogant smile with fire in her eyes. But the smile only widened, and his left eyebrow arched. "Well. . ." he said slowly, "I know you love surprises, hate eating alone, don't take phone calls while you're working, and you're allergic to strawberries. Shall I go on?"

Stunned, feeling enraged and somehow violated, Paige could do nothing but grip the chair and let her mouth fall open. Before she could think of the next move, he walked toward her, shoved the pillow at her, and headed for the door, where he paused and turned. "And I know you didn't answer David's question when he asked if you'd prayed about this."

When she could think enough to move, she walked into the hallway, threw the pillow down next to her canvas bag, and headed for the back door and fresh air. Before she got there, she ran into Robert. He gave her a rueful smile.

"Guess I should have found a better place for Brant to take a nap, huh? He was up all night on call, and then just after he got back from transporting a patient for us this afternoon he got another Flight-for-Life call. I told him to sack out on the couch when he got back; I didn't think he was in any condition to drive home. But it sounds like he was having a fairly lively discussion with you instead of sleeping."

Paige's clenched jaws slackened. "I guess you could call it that," she said, then added slowly, "I saw that accident. . .how can anyone deal with that day after day?"

Robert nodded. "It takes a toll. Makes a person a little irritable at times, too, I imagine." He smiled at her. "Go on out and get some fresh air. You look like you could use it."

Outside, Paige took a deep breath and pressed her hands against her hot cheeks. She sucked in another breath, and then went back inside.

Two double A batteries sat on top of her pillow in the hallway. She was touched by David's thoughtfulness, but there was no way she could paint now.

nine

Sleep was the only thing on Brant's mind as he parked his pickup next to the house. He wanted to close his eyes and erase the last few hours.

He'd been in a foul mood ever since the last accident. Some things you got used to; you learned to wall off your emotions so that cries of pain and the sight of mangled bodies didn't pierce your soul anymore. They were part of the job. But there was no way to harden yourself against what he'd seen today. You never got used to the death of a child.

Had it not been for the accident, he knew he would have responded differently to Paige. He probably would have kept his opinion to himself in the first place. They'd gotten off on the wrong foot from the moment he'd laid eyes on her, and he had a feeling there wasn't much he could do to change it. That fact only added to the darkness that hovered over him like a thunderhead.

The last thing he needed now was another reminder of loss, but that was exactly what was waiting for him, tucked behind the screen door in a thick brown envelope. The package fell on his foot when he walked in. Knowing immediately what it was, he kicked it out of the way and walked up the three steps leading into the kitchen.

He dropped onto a plastic-cushioned chair and slowly unlaced his boots. Too numb to construct words, his mind formed pictures into prayers. He saw the young mother standing alone by the side of the freeway, sinking to her knees in grief. He saw her husband, strapped to a back board, being lifted into the helicopter, reaching out to the covered body of his son.

Tears filled Brant's eyes and he rested his head in his hands and let them fall. He'd long since learned not to ask "why?" but the question that came through the fog of his exhaustion was "how?" How, in the face of such grief, do you survive, how do you put one foot in front of the other, or even take the next breath without the Lord?

He stepped into the shower and turned the water as hot as he could stand it. It pelted his chest with fiery needles, making his skin red. Then, gradually, he lowered the temperature, cooling down until the water felt icy against his back. It was a strange ritual, he supposed, a kind of purging, but it did wonders for the tension in his muscles and the heaviness in his spirit.

He put on a pair of cut-off sweatpants and walked out to the kitchen. He grabbed a soda out of the refrigerator and pulled a jar of peanut butter and a package of crackers from the cupboard. As he unscrewed the jar lid, he glanced down the steps to the back door. The padded envelope stared up at him from the floor, taunting him. He stared back as he spread peanut butter on a cracker and chewed it slowly. He went through half a roll of crackers that way, his eyes still on the package, an imaginary conversation going on in his head. Before he picked it up, he had to be ready with a defense, even though, as always, he'd be the only one to hear it.

He put the crackers away, downed the last of the soda, and turned to the bedroom. The package could wait until morning. Or longer.

He was sound asleep within sixty seconds. For over an hour he was dead to the world, but the phone rang just before ten and woke him. He didn't have a phone in the bedroom and he didn't have an answering machine; if he got up, whoever it was would have hung up by the time he got to the living room. He rolled over and pulled the pillow over his head. His pager was on the night stand; in the event of an emergency, he could be reached.

But as hard as he tried to clear his mind, sleep would not return. He was plagued with a gnawing sense that he'd left something undone. When he finally quit fighting the feeling and prayed about it, two images flashed in his mind simultaneously. One was the envelope on the floor by the back door. The other was Paige, clutching her pillow, her deep brown eyes flashing at him, cutting him. And suddenly, in the dark room with his eyes closed, he saw what he had missed in his anger: the hurt that she had tried to mask in defensiveness. He thought of the envelope. Maybe he and the girl with the pearls on her fingernails were not so different after all.

He got up and put on a T-shirt. As he slipped into his sandals at the back door, he thought about calling first, but decided against it. If Cody wasn't there, Brant had a key. As he bent down and picked up the envelope, he said out loud, "Ah, the wonders of modern technology. Video parenting—it's the wave of the future, folks! So much more convenient than the old days of Super 8 Movie parenting!" He wondered what his parents would say if they knew he didn't even own a VCR, that he hadn't owned one the whole time he lived in Canada. Every time they'd sent a tape he'd had to watch it at the ranger station thirty miles from his cabin, usually with half a dozen other guys hanging around.

He knew he was being childish. But wasn't that their fault? Didn't kids get psychologically stuck at some immature level if their emotional needs weren't met? Not that he'd grown up without love, he'd had plenty of it. But it hadn't come from where he needed it most. It was hard to soak in love from someone else when your own parents were strangers. When he and his sister were little, "Mom and Dad" had been the people on the movie screen in Gramma and Grampa's basement. They were still down there, reels and reels of "Mom and Dad," all neatly labeled: "Jane and Warren in Peru," "Jane and Warren in Guatamala," "Jane and Warren—Christmas in Mexico City". . . He sometimes wondered what kind of a parent he'd make without having had good roll models. But at least he knew the most important thing—he'd be there.

He prayed as he drove. It was the only way to divert the sarcasm that kept bubbling to the surface. "Forgive me, Lord. You know I don't want this bitterness. Help me to love them. Their eyes are blind without You, they have no idea how they hurt us."

The door was locked when he got to Cody's house, so he let himself in. He had no secrets from his best friend, but still he was glad to be alone. These "visits" with his parents were more painful than he wanted to admit, and it was just easier to handle with no one else around.

He took his sandals off and walked barefoot across the teal carpeting. He smiled to himself as he looked around. There were new curtains in the kitchen. It would only be a bachelor pad for a few more days, and Hailey's subtle touches were already evident.

Brant felt a bit wistful thinking about it; it was the close of an era that he and Cody had made last far longer than either of them could have predicted. Just being in the little bungalow brought back so many memories, even though it had been completely redecorated since the days when they had used it as their "secret hideaway."

As he popped the tape in the VCR and settled on the floor in front of the couch, he realized he hadn't even glanced at the post mark. He wondered cynically what rain forest or mountain top they'd be on this time.

But this was something different. His father sat behind a desk, while his mother, in a skirt and jacket instead of the usual khakis and T-shirt, sat on the corner of the desk. Through the window behind them stretched a city skyline. His mother, her silver hair actually permed, spoke first. "Surprise! Bet you never thought you'd see us like this, did you? We're in Los Angeles!"

The picture zoomed in on his father, and Brant suddenly realized that there was someone operating the camera. Had they always done that? Somehow he'd always pictured the camera sitting on a tripod. It struck his tired mind as bizarre and made him want to laugh out loud.

"We're heading into our biggest project yet, Brant. Starting our own magazine! It's about time, huh? Thought you'd like the idea since you're always talking about going into business for yourself! We're calling it *Sea to Sea*. Catchy, huh? Going to focus on the natural wonders of the U.S.; little-known places, not the usual tourist traps. We'll target environmentalists and the back-to-nature types. Lots of pictures, you know."

The camera shifted again. "And that's where you come

in! There's a place in this company just tailor-made for you! You'd have your own plane and be your own boss . . .well almost!" She gave a little-girl giggle; it was not becoming on a sixty-three-year-old woman. "You'd have to answer to us, of course, but that's the next best thing to being your own boss!"

The cameraman panned back to his father. Brant wondered if they were following a script. "Always knew that pilot's license of yours would come in handy some day, son!"

Son. Brant hadn't realized that he'd been digging his fingers into the thick teal carpet until the word made his hands clench. His father laughed and spread his hands in front of him. "We need aerial shots, you know? And we need to be able to be on the move at the drop of a hat. We need a cracker-jack pilot who likes living on the edge; someone who really wants to make a difference in the world. We'd be proud to have you work with us, son!"

At that moment, Cody walked in the back door and ambled into the living room. Brant picked up the VCR controls and paused the video just as the cameraman backed up and got them both on the screen. Cody, who had sat through hours of the McCourts' travelogs over the years, gave Brant a sympathetic look. "Hi, Mom. Hi, Dad. Where's the jungle?"

"Don't ask."

"Want a soda?"

"Sure."

Brant waited until Cody flopped down on the couch behind him before pushing play. "How 'bout it?" his mother asked. "Isn't this just perfect for you, Brant? You could have the whole downstairs of our condo, you'd be right in the city, but you'd still get to enjoy nature. And like your father said, this is a chance to leave your mark on the world, to do something really worthwhile with your life. Have you sold the farm yet?"

His father leaned forward. "Don't worry about it. I know a developer from Chicago that would lap that up in a min—" Brant snapped off the picture.

Cody shook his head. "I have no idea what that was all about, but I totally agree with them. It's about time you quit saving lives and start doing something worthwhile with your life, son!"

Brant pointed the VCR controls at Cody and pushed stop.

ten

The next morning, the throbbing inside Paige's head woke her long before the alarm went off. She had spent most of the night replaying first David's words and then Brant's. Over and over she had tried to convince herself that, while David's opinion mattered, the opinion of an egotistical stranger was meaningless. But every time she closed her eyes she saw the look on Brant's face as he'd walked out of the room.

Something else gnawed at her as she walked to the bathroom, trying to rub the knots out of her neck, but she couldn't think what it was. She opened the door of the medicine cabinet, hunting for something to relieve her headache, then slammed it again when she found nothing. Sitting on the edge of the bath tub, she opened a bottle of bath gel, then lit a strawberry-scented candle. *Strawberries.* How did he know she was allergic to strawberries?

Pinning her hair up high on her head, she stepped into the tub and sank into the bubbles. As she forced her mind to concentrate on the mural she had to start, Mrs. Patches pushed open the door that hadn't quite latched and leaped onto the edge of the tub, where she began playfully swatting at the bubbles with her right paw. Scooping a handful of bubbles, Paige deposited them on top of Mrs. Patches' head and laughed as she bent her ear with her paw, trying to get them off. Gradually, the distraction and the heat eased her tension and the headache subsided.

Leaning back, she yawned and closed her eyes, trying to picture a zebra, but seeing, once again, Brant's face. The thoughts of the night resurfaced, floating through her mind like the bubbles on the water. Never had anyone made her feel so explosive, so out of control and vulnerable. She was unaccustomed to feeling herself an open book. She couldn't count the number of times a date had called her "mysterious," a quality she had enjoyed and actually cultivated. Now suddenly this man she didn't even like was staring through her, reading her. She tried to reason that he could have gotten his facts from Hailey or Cody, but the truth of it finally pushed to the surface: Brant McCourt knew things about her that she hadn't even admitted to herself.

Hailey called from work just as Paige was pouring her first cup of coffee. "There's a note for you on the porch," she said.

Paige took a sip of coffee. "Okay."

"Go read it."

"Why don't you just tell me what it says. Save me walking all that way."

"I don't know what it says! Why do you think I'm calling?"

"Didn't you write it?"

"No. I was going down to let the cat out about five this morning when it. . .arrived."

"It 'arrived'? By what. . .car, truck, carrier pigeon?"

"On foot. . .kind of."

"Make sense, girl."

"Go read it."

Paige was already halfway out the door with the cordless phone. Sitting on the round wicker table on the porch was an ivory parchment envelope with her name stenciled on it in gold letters. "Okay, I've got it."

"Well? What's it say? Hurry up! My break's almost over!"

Paige smiled. "Mmm. . .I know how you love a good mystery! I think I'll have to sit down for this one. Let's see. . .the rocker, the chair, or the bench? Which would be most comfortable?"

"Read it!"

Yawning loudly, Paige sat down, opened the envelope, and pulled out a card in matching parchment. "Okay, let's see. . .my, what pretty stenciling. Someone went through a great deal of trouble just for me. It says 'Dear Paige, How about a bit of lunch with me at The Greenhouse at 1:00 this afternoon? I look forward to seeing you.'"

"'How about a bit of lunch?' That's weird!"

"Haven't you read Winnie the Pooh?"

"Not recently."

"Well, that's what Pooh's always having—a bit of lunch." Paige frowned. "The card's not signed. Who brought it?"

"Well, I want to tell you, but I think it's supposed to be a surprise, but I know you and I know that you're going to be thinking all morning that it's some secret admirer and then you're going to get all dressed up and then you're going to be disappointed when you find out it's only. . ."

"Only who?"

"Oh. . ." Hailey whined. "You have to promise not to tell him that I told you and you have to promise to act surprised."

"I promise."

"Well, it was the weirdest thing. The cat started stepping on my face so I finally got up to let her out and I heard a car door slam out on the road as I was coming down the stairs, and just as I opened the door to the porch, the outside door closed and there was. . .this guy . . .running around the corner of the house."

"Did you recognize him?"

There was a pause on Hailey's end and then a quiet, "Yes."

Paige sighed. "Spit it out! Your break's almost over, remember?"

"You're right. Bye."

"Hailey! I'll hurt you!"

"Oh, this is such a cool thing! Why can't it be some tall, dark, and handsome guy that you'd fall madly in love with? I mean, he was—tall, dark, and handsome—well, maybe not exactly dark, but—"

Picking up the silver whistle that Hailey had taped to the phone for prank calls, Paige let out a long, steady blast, not loud enough to hurt Hailey's ear, but enough to shut her up.

"Okay!" There was another long pause. "It was Robert."

After her initial disappointment had faded, Paige began to address the obvious question, and the only probable answer sent her flying back to her room to change out of painting clothes and into shopping clothes. It was her philosophy that every celebration was cause for a new outfit.

The phone rang as she was ready to walk out the door. "May I please speak to Miss Paige Stern?" said the voice in her ear when she picked up the receiver.

"Speaking."

"This is Sandy from The Greenhouse. I'm calling to confirm your one o'clock reservation."

Paige smiled smugly, "Tell Dr. Worth I'll be there with bells on!"

ぁ

Paige's right hand smoothed out the wrinkles in the rose-printed napkin on her lap. It was ten after one and still no sign of Robert. It crossed her mind just once as she tried to relax against the chintz-covered chair, that she could have been wrong about the purpose of this meeting, but she dismissed the doubt as quickly as it surfaced. Surely he wouldn't pick such a cheerful setting to dash her hopes.

The Greenhouse had just opened in June and this was the first time Paige had been here. Her artistic eye quickly approved the interior design. The round tables were covered with pastel tablecloths and in the center of each one was a glass bowl filled with clear marbles and a simple arrangement of irises, daffodils, and tulips. The walls were stenciled to depict a flower garden in full bloom, and baskets of flowers and trailing vines hung from trellises mounted on the ceiling. Several sky lights flooded the room with natural light and reminded Paige of lunching *alfresco* at her favorite café in Paris.

Her thoughts were interrupted by the voice of the host who had seated her almost twenty minutes earlier. "Miss Stern? Your luncheon date phoned to say he's terrible sorry but he has been unfortunately detained, but he said you should order if you wish."

She hesitated; she hated eating alone. Reluctantly, she picked up the menu and smiled at the host. "I'm used to being stood up," she quipped.

The man in the black vest stared at her in open admiration, his eyes traveling from her sleek black hair to the white linen dress embroidered with gold tropical fish. The dress had spaghetti straps and it's straight lines fell softly to mid-calf with a small slit up the left side. He bowed slightly, in very European fashion. "I sincerely doubt that, ma'am."

Paige offered a smile in return for the compliment. She ordered and told the waiter that she would be in the gift shop.

The small shop adjacent to the restaurant was an actual greenhouse, filled with plants, books, cards, plaques, and knickknacks. It smelled of wet dirt, scented candles, and potpourri. Paige found a tiny Green Bay Packer T-shirt that she couldn't resist picking up for Jordan and a copy of *Mr. Jeremy Fisher*, one of the few Beatrix Potter stories she didn't have in her collection. The book would be her first purchase for Annie's room.

Her salad had arrived when she got back to the table. Holding *Mr. Jeremy Fisher* in one hand, she pierced a cherry tomato with her fork and stuck it, whole, in her mouth. Just as she did, a voice behind her said, "Ah. . . 'are we having roasted grasshopper with ladybug sauce? Frogs consider it a beautiful treat, but I think it would have been awful!' "

With her fork still clamped firmly between her lips, she stared up at the man next to her. She didn't even pretend a smile as he took off his mirrored sunglasses and laid them on the table, then took off the blue and orange jacket with the paramedic emblem on the front and laid it on the back of the chair across from her.

Picking up the book, he said, "My grandmother used to

read this to me. I knew the whole thing by heart."

Paige took the fork out of her mouth and laid it carefully and deliberately next to her plate. "Obviously," she said.

He leafed through several pages. "You draw better than this; they should have asked you to illustrate it."

If there was one thing she couldn't stand, it was being patronized. Instead of thanking him, she said, "What are you doing here?"

"Oh. . .I know the guy that bought this place. Cody and I went to high school with him. Nice, huh? Are you waiting for someone?"

"Yes."

He waited for more of an answer; and when none came, he asked, "Who?"

Paige gritted her teeth. "Dr. Worth."

"Mmm. Mind if I sit down until he gets here?"

Reluctantly, she said, "No."

The waiter walked up and set a glass in front of Brant and filled it from a pitcher, then handed him a menu, asking, "Would you like a few minutes?"

Brant shook his head. Handing the menu back, he said, "I'll have the beef stew and a salad with Thousand Island; just water to drink."

Paige's mouth opened in what was becoming a familiar expression whenever Brant was around. He smiled. "You don't mind if I have a bit of lunch with you?"

As her jaw dropped even lower, he reached into his jacket and pulled out a thin branch about six inches long with small green leaves. At the end of the branch was a peach satin ribbon. He handed it to her. Paige took it, touching first the leaves, then the ribbon, then lifting her gaze to his, asked the question with her eyes.

"It's boxwood. I couldn't find an olive tree." He stared at her with a look that made the branch tremble in her hand.

"It's a peace offering; I was out of line yesterday."

Paige fingered the shiny leaves, strangely touched by the simplicity and creativity of his offering. A dozen roses would not have swayed her, but this tiny branch had completely disarmed her. "Thank you," she said quietly.

"Does that mean I'm forgiven?"

She smiled at him and nodded. He extended his hand toward her across the table. "Friends?" When she hesitated for a fraction of a second he said, "Potentially?"

Paige laughed and held out her hand. "Potential friends. I like that."

"Are you always up before five?" he asked out of the blue.

"I'm never up before five! Why?"

"I assumed you saw Robert delivering my message."

"Hailey saw him." Paige took her time pulling apart a hard roll and taking a bite. What she wanted to say sounded too intimate. Her impression of Brant was changing much too fast and she wasn't sure she wanted to risk being mere feed for what she had assumed was his colossal ego. In the end, though, she said the words anyway. "I love surprises."

"I know."

"The card was very creative."

"I bought the paint and stencils for a bike I'm working on. Thought it would add a touch of intrigue. By the way, did the batteries work?"

"You left them?"

"Mmm-hm."

The waiter brought their food then and Brant said, "I'll pray." His prayer was simple, but so much from the heart that it made Paige oddly uncomfortable

"I'm sorry I was so late," he said. "I wasn't supposed to be on call today, but you know how that works. Are you disappointed that the invitation wasn't from Robert?"

Paige hesitated. An honest answer would require some explanation. "I was hoping that David had talked to Robert and that Robert was going to give me his blessing to start adoption proceedings."

Brant nodded. "I'm sorry if I misled you."

"I shouldn't have let myself think like that." She looked at him, wondering what had happened to the ice she had seen in his eyes the first time she met him. "You still think I'm wrong, don't you?"

"I'm not sure I have a right to voice my opinion."

"I think potential friends have that right."

Brant smiled. "I don't want to end the way we did yesterday."

"We won't."

"We might." He took a drink of water, set the glass down, and ran his finger up and down the cut-glass side of the goblet. "It's not my style to soft-pedal things."

"So I've noticed. I'm a big girl, Mr. McCourt. I'll listen, then make up my own mind."

Brant stared at her, then at his watch, and sighed. "I have to be back at the station in twenty minutes. This isn't turning out the way I'd intended. I thought we'd have more time just to get to know each other, and I promised myself I wouldn't touch the subject of Annie today. What are you doing tomorrow afternoon?"

"I'm distracting T.J. and Shelly so David and Karlee can have some quiet time alone with the baby. I promised Annie I'd take her along so she could ride T.J.'s pony, and then we're all going back to my place to watch *101 Dalmatians*. Would you like to join us?"

"Not exactly what I had in mind for our first date, but I'll take it. What are you doing Friday night?"

"I don't know. But I have a feeling you're about to tell me."

"How about your first lesson, then a moonlight flight and dinner?"

"Sounds wonderful." She picked up the branch and turned it over in her hand. Looking up at him, she said, "We just might end up being friends after all."

eleven

Paige balanced on the top bar of the split-rail fence with T.J. on one side of her and Shelly on the other. "I don't think he's ridden horses much," T.J. observed.

"I think you're right, Teej," Paige answered, snapping a picture.

"What if he drops Annie?" Shelly added.

Paige waved at Annie and watched her dark curls bouncing against Brant's blue denim shirt. "Blacky's just walking; there's no danger. . .I hope."

Shelly looked nervously at the pony, then back at Paige. "Isn't it time to go to your house now?"

"Yeah, I guess it is." She motioned for Brant to steer Blacky in their direction. With T.J. snickering on one side and Shelly holding her breath on the other, she had a hard time maintaining a neutral face when he finally reached them. She held her arms out to a reluctant Annie. "Want to go to my house and watch a movie?"

Annie's head bobbed up and down and she dove into Paige's arms. She waved at the pony. "Bye, Bwacky!"

Paige rubbed her nose on Annie's cheek. "Should we make popcorn at my house?"

"Uh-huh. Can Bwacky have po-corn?"

"I don't think so."

"Why?"

"I don't think he likes popcorn."

"Why?"

" 'Cause horses eat oats and hay."

"Why?"

She was saved from answering when T.J. burst out laughing beside her. When she saw what he was laughing at, she put her hand over his mouth and wished she had a free hand for her own. Brant was trying to turn Blacky away from the fence. What Brant hadn't seen, but Blacky obviously had, was the apple in T.J.'s closed fist.

Giving up, Brant ungracefully dismounted and caught them laughing. "Go ahead and have your fun now," he said. "Just wait 'til I get you three thousand feet in the air and hand you the reins!" He turned on his heel and walked into the barn.

The next sound they heard from him was, "Youch!"

T.J ran into the barn and came running out just as fast. "Paige! Come quick! He's bleeding all over the place!"

Paige felt every nerve ending in the small of her back. She set Annie down outside the fence. "Take her into the house, Shel." Seeing the fear on her niece's face, she added, "You know how T.J. exaggerates." But as she jumped down, Brant walked out, his left hand clamped over his right. Blood was on his shirt and running between his fingers.

Taking a deep breath, Paige put on a competent act. "Let's get you into the house," she said, opening the gate for him.

"It's not as bad as it looks. I don't want to drip blood all over the house. Where's the hose?" Paige felt her stomach lurch, but Brant went on talking. "I couldn't see in the dark and I caught the side of my hand on a nail. It ripped a chunk of skin off, but it's not deep."

Small black spots appeared in front of Paige's eyes. She wasn't sure if she was still walking, but Brant kept talking. "I'm current on my tetanus shots, so I don't have to worry about that." He stopped and turned to her as T.J. handed him the hose and ran to turn it on. "If you could just get me a couple of—whoa!" He grabbed her and eased her to the step of the deck. "Put your head down!" The hose came on and he pulled his shirt off and soaked it with water, then wrung it out and put it on the back of her neck, then wiped her face with it.

After several minutes, she felt the blood returning to her head and she looked up. Brant had his hand wrapped in his shirt and there was no blood to be seen. He grinned at her. "I've been a paramedic for a long time, but I've never seen anyone turn quite that color before."

Paige groaned and pointed to his hand. "Is it bad?"

"No. Wanna see?"

"No!" Paige put her hand over her face. "This is so embarrassing!"

T.J. came with the first-aid kit and Brant began unwrapping his hand. Grinning again, he looked a Paige. "Want to give me a hand with this?"

"Stop it!"

T.J. opened the red and white box and sat down on the step. "I'll help you," he said. "Girls are wimps." Paige covered her face with her hands, but Brant slowly peeled one hand away. "We all have our weaknesses," he said softly.

"You don't. 'Cept you don't ride very well."

Brant laughed. "Well, I have a few other weaknesses besides. Ask Cody about me and road kill sometime."

❧

On Monday afternoon when she came home from the Gallery, Paige found a note from Hailey on the counter. "Robert wants to talk to you when you have time. I don't know what it's about, but this time it's really him!"

Paige flew to the phone, but the tone of his voice as he talked to her let her know that he did not have good news. An hour later she stood in his office listening to something that wasn't sinking in. She couldn't let it.

"He has a right to see his daughter," Robert repeated softly.

"And she has a right to be raised by someone who loves her and understands her, not some freak whose face is plastered over every tabloid in the country!"

"He may not even want her, Paige."

"But if he does? A biological act doesn't make him a father! Robert, did you ever listen to his lyrics? They're so corrupt! He's an atheist and a drug addict! And how do we know he didn't know about her until a month ago? Maybe he knew all along and didn't care!"

Even to her own ears, her voice sounded harsh after Robert's gentle words. Robert settled on the corner of his desk, facing her, and motioned once again for her to sit down. Feeling like a school child, she finally complied, looking up at the thick, snowy-white hair, the strong, tanned face that denied his sixty-four years. His eyes looked tired, but the kindness in them was never dimmed by fatigue. He turned the pen in his hand over, end to end, several times, seemingly engrossed in the action, then cleared his throat. "Can I play the father figure here for a minute?"

Paige gave a weak smile and swiped at a stray tear,

then nodded.

"Let's just say for a minute that Roman decides to relinquish his rights. I don't know how much you've actually looked into this, but you could face some huge problems in the adoption process. You're single and Caucasian—adopting a bi-racial child can be difficult. Some people feel strongly that a child should be raised by someone who shares her ethnic heritage."

"But with her disabilities. . ."

"I know. I just want you to be aware that there could be problems. Okay, let's say that all the road blocks are removed. I hope you'll believe that I'm not trying to stand in your way, only that I want to be sure that you know what you're facing. I know you've seen Annie at her worst and I also know that you're as good with her as anyone on staff, but. . ." He stared at her, knowing his words would seem strong and hurtful, but unable to avoid them. "You've only been with her for a few hours at a time. Twenty-four hours, seven days a week with a child like this can seem interminable. . .especially for someone with no parenting experience. And what would you do about work?"

"As of the first of August I'll be the manager of the Gallery. That means a raise and also that I'm in charge of scheduling—and the assistant manager has kids at home and she's interested in job sharing. Annie can be here in day school half-days until she's. . .if and when she's ready for kindergarten. I've really thought it through."

Robert nodded. "What about time for yourself? For painting and travel and all the things you're used to doing?"

Paige stared down at her hands. This was the only area

she hadn't completely resolved, but she wasn't about to let on. "I've lived in Paris, traveled all over Europe, spent a summer with David and Shawna in Senegal, and seen most of the U.S. and Canada." She attempted a convincing smile. "I think I've got it out of my system. And I could paint after Annie was in bed."

"If you had the energy left." It was not a sarcastic comment, simply the truth, Paige realized, but she had thought it through, she assured him again. Robert nodded. "What about relationships. . .dating?"

"I couldn't be interested in anyone who couldn't accept Annie."

"Is that fair? A lot of men are hesitant about getting interested in a woman with a child, and for good reasons."

"You weren't."

Robert smiled. "Touché. But Cody's mother was a patient and then a friend for years before I married her."

"But it can be done."

"Yes, it can."

"Marriage isn't for everyone anyway."

"True. Some people are called to be single. Do you think that's your calling, Paige?"

Paige looked away. "Maybe I should just hold a press conference so I can tell everyone at once! No, I don't think I'm called to be single! But I don't think I'm called to get married until the right guy comes along! What if he doesn't show up until I'm too old to have kids?"

With only a hint of a smile, Robert said, "Don't you think God can read your biological clock?"

"I suppose, but—" The buzzer on Robert's phone interrupted her.

"I'm sorry," he said, turning around to push the button.

Charissa's voice answered. "Mrs. Welch is here."

Paige stood and Robert reached out to give her a fatherly hug. "Whether you like it or not I'm going to be praying for your future husband. And there's something I want you to pray about."

"What's that?"

"Roman Slayder will be here Friday night. I'd like you to be here. I believe that you know Annie better than anyone here. I trust you to be honest in spite of your own desires, and I also trust you to be objective."

"Objective?"

"About Roman. He has his rights and we will not interfere. . .unless Annie's health and safety appear to be in jeopardy."

ᴣᴀ

Friday came much faster than she would have liked. It had been a hectic week, with the Gallery's manager being rushed off for an emergency appendectomy on Tuesday, and two of the college students employed by the Gallery away on an art class trip. What it had meant for Paige was being there an hour before opening until an hour after closing each day.

After locking up on Friday evening, she kicked off her shoes and carried them to her car. Her feet hurt, her back ached, and instead of the planned moonlight flight with Brant, she had to meet the famous Roman Slayder. It was the last thing in the world she wanted to do.

Taking the scenic back roads instead of I-90 would lengthen the drive to the Sparrow Center to forty-five minutes and give her time to unwind. She prayed out loud for the first fifteen miles, pleading her case before the highest court. But as she turned onto a rustic road just north of Cambridge, the words stopped and, for the first time in a very long time, she began to listen. What she heard in the silence as she passed through the stretched-thin tree shadows on the country road was not a voice, but a conviction, a conviction that the focus of her pleas should not be Annie, nor herself, but Roman Slayder. It was a conviction she did not welcome.

The helicopter was in the field behind the employee parking lot, casting a monstrous shadow on the grass. As she slammed the car door, Paige had the strange sensation that she was acting out a scene from one of Hailey's mystery novels. The helicopter, the near-empty parking lot, the odd hour for visitors, all carefully planned to avoid media attention and keep fans off Roman Slayder's trail. Quaestor was in Minneapolis for a Saturday concert and Roman had been flown by private plane from a small town just outside the Twin Cities to the Madison airport where Brant had picked him up in the helicopter. To avoid the possibility of being seen, Robert had even invited Roman to spend the night at his house. Unlocking the back door with the key Robert had loaned her, she wondered cynically if she'd be met by a guard with a metal detector.

Instead, she was met by total silence. Robert had scheduled a skeleton crew of one LPN, two trusted aids, himself, and Hailey. Hailey would be covering the intensive care nursery and Paige assumed she'd find Robert and Annie in the day room. As she walked down the hall, her heels making light clicks on the vinyl, she wondered if they had gotten Annie to take an afternoon nap. If not, her father's first impression would probably not be favorable.

Absorbed in her thoughts, she jumped at the sight of

another person. "Marsella!" The head of the housekeeping department was changing a light bulb in one of the brass wall fixtures that were only turned on at night.

"Miss Stern!" the woman gasped, as startled as Paige. "You like to 'lectrocute me!"

Paige laughed. "I'm sorry! I was just surprised to see you here so late."

"My car. She breaks down on my way and I have to wait for my son to fix it. Tomorrow is my vacation; I am going home to see my mother! But I have things to finish here first. So. . ." She gave a shrug and smiled. "So I stay late. You are late, too. Art classes at night?"

Paige thought fast. "No. I'm on my way home from the Gallery. I stopped by to talk with Dr. Worth. Maybe we can go out and get some pie and coffee later. He works too much."

Marsella nodded. "So does Mr. McCourt. Felicia says he brought a patient in tonight. Very late for admitting a patient, isn't it?"

Paige shrugged, as casually as she could. "Well, have a wonderful trip and don't work too hard tonight, Marsella."

"You should take me out for pie and coffee I think!"

Paige laughed. "I'll do that! As soon as you get back!"

She opened the door to the day room. The scene on the other side of the door was so different from what she'd expected that it took a minute to register. Sitting on the floor, cross-legged, in boots, faded jeans, a forest green shirt, leather vest, and a tightly curled hot-pink wig, was Brant McCourt. He looked up at her, smiled, and said, "Laugh and you die."

As Paige clamped her hand over her mouth, Annie ran up and wrapped around her knees. "I maked Mr. 'Court pretty!" she said proudly.

"Yes, Annie. You made Mr. McCourt very pretty! But I think he needs a hat and a purse, don't you? Can you find a purse and a very big hat for Mr. McCourt?"

As Annie ran across the room to the costume box, Paige pulled a small chair away from the table and sat down facing Brant. "Pretty in pink," she said. "How'd you end up with this job?"

"One of the kids had a convulsion. He's okay, but it woke up the whole room so every available hand is settling kids. Since I'm better at dress-up than lullabies, I volunteered for this. Robert is in his office with 'Rock Star Dad' going over Annie's file. Robert wanted him to be as prepared as possible."

"What's he like?"

Brant took time out to tickle Annie as she set a huge, floppy hat on his head, then sent her off in search of one for Paige. "Nothing like I expected. He asked a lot about the Center, and we talked about the Packers and how he grew up in Milwaukee. He may have a ring in his nose and dreadlocks down to his waist, but he's just a regular guy! I was prepared to dislike him, but he's not the creep I thought he'd be."

Neither are you, Paige thought. Annie held out a six-gallon cowboy hat and Paige bent over so Annie could put it on her head. "Yee-ha! Ride 'em cowboy!" Paige said, slapping her thigh and sending Annie into a fit of giggles.

"She's a neat kid," Brant said. "How are you handling this?"

"Part of me would like to sabotage this whole thing, but God had a little talk with me on the way over here."

Brant smiled. "The still, small voice. What did He say?"

"That this isn't about me. It's about Roman."

Brant reached up and grabbed her hand. "Let's pray before he comes in."

twelve

As Brant prayed, his pink-wigged head bowed, Annie put on a sombrero with dangling tassels and slipped a yellow plastic gun into Paige's free hand. . .and Robert led Roman Slayder into the room. Still holding Paige's hand, Brant stood, pulled Paige to her feet, and without hesitation did a smooth, graceful curtsey. Robert, having dreaded this moment, could have hugged the man in the pink curls for breaking the ice.

Robert introduced Paige, then, following Roman's eyes, said, "And this is Anika. We call her Annie." Annie started to walk toward him, but Paige instinctively bent and scooped her up.

"Hey," Roman said by way of greeting, then shifted his weight from one foot to the other. Paige tightened her hold on Annie, knowing full well she was giving the child non-verbal cues. "I brought you somethin'," he said, producing a wrapped box from behind his back.

He's trying to buy her! The thought blared in her head and she locked eyes with Robert, who read her thoughts loud and clear and returned a look of understanding with just a hint of warning. Once again, she felt like the defiant child and wanted nothing more than to bolt for the door with Annie in her arms and run for all she was worth.

Annie's dark eyes lit and she slid out of Paige's arms, took the package, and sat on the floor at their feet, tearing at the paper. Roman stared down at her, still shifting from left to right. The ringed fingers of his right hand played with the silver medallion that hung from a chain around his neck. Annie struggled with the package, ripping off most of the bright paper, but she was unable to budge the tight ribbon that crossed all four sides.

Robert smiled at Roman. "Looks like she could use some help."

"Yeah. . .sure." He crouched beside her, producing a mother-of-pearl-handled pocket knife that sent chills down Paige's back as it slipped through the ribbon like a razor blade. Annie lifted the lid and pulled out a drum the size of a large coffee can and stared at it, then at the man across from her. Once again, Robert stepped in. "Maybe Mr. Slayder can show you how to use it, Annie."

Paige's hands drew into fists. *Why don't we just write him an instruction book? The Care and Feeding of Little Girls—for Fathers Who Really Don't Care Anyway.* She glared at Robert again. Wasn't it obvious to him that this man didn't have a clue? Roman settled cross-legged on the floor and began tapping his fingertips on the rawhide. Annie stared, mesmerized, until he stopped. Then, slowly, she reached out and tapped, first one hand, then two, and then there was no stopping her.

Robert and Brant perched on the edge of a low table to watch. Paige turned the little chair around and sat down. The braids in Annie's hair bounced, the colored balls on her hair bands making a soft clacking noise. Suddenly, the pounding stopped and Annie pointed to Roman. It took him a minute to understand her meaning, but this time he looked at her instead of helplessly to Robert. Catching on, he played a simple beat, then stopped, pointing back at her. Annie copied his rhythm, beat for beat, flawlessly. And Paige felt like something was slipping through her fingers.

❧

When she walked out of Annie's room and down the hall to Robert's office, she felt drained, her back ached, and she knew she was dangerously close to tears. She was in no condition to be talking to Roman. Stopping outside Robert's door, she ran her fingers through her hair, adjusted her wide red belt, and brushed her hands against the skirt of the black shirt-waist dress she'd put on seventeen hours earlier. Just when she felt almost presentable, she heard footsteps behind her.

"Missing something, Miss Stern?"

She turned around to see her black heels dangling from Brant's fingertips. She stared at him blankly, then down at her stockinged feet. "You left them in the day room." Smiling at her as she slipped into the shoes, he reached out and put his hands behind her neck. Her tired mind glided in slow-motion to the conclusion that he was going to hug her, but thankfully her reflexes were just as slow. She laughed, uncharacteristically embarrassed, as he unfastened a string of purple plastic beads, pulled them off her neck, and slipped them into his shirt pocket. "You look exhausted," he said softly, "but can I ask a favor?"

Paige nodded, responding to both his question and his observation.

"Could you give me a ride home? My truck is at the airport."

"Sure. But I don't know how long this will take."

"No prob. You know where to find me."

"My pillow is in the cupboard behind the door."

"Thanks. I'll be praying for you. This won't be easy."

As she turned toward the office, she wondered momentarily what she would have done if he *had* been trying to put his arms around her.

Robert sat behind the desk, leaning forward on his elbows, his shirt sleeves rolled up. Paige took the swivel chair next to Roman and looked at Robert. He cleared his throat. "I've given Roman as much medical information as possible, and I've filled him in on Annie's history and daily routine. I thought you could—"

A voice shouted over the intercom on his desk. "Dr. Worth, Brandon is seizing again!"

"I'll be right there." He looked apologetically at Roman as he rose from his chair, then almost pleadingly at Paige. It was a look that plainly said, "Be nice."

Yes, Daddy, she wanted to say, but she silenced the sarcastic little voice inside her. She turned to Roman, knowing full well what was expected of her, and disobeyed. "So, is it true you didn't know you had a daughter until last month?"

Roman looked over her right shoulder. "I haven't seen her mother since I moved to California. I had no idea she was pregnant when I left."

"Must have been quite a surprise. Do you have other children?"

For the first time, his eyes met hers. "I suppose the answer you're expecting is 'not that I know of'." He leaned forward, never taking his eyes from hers. "Miss Stern, don't believe everything you read."

Not one to blush easily, Paige was startled by the warmth creeping up her neck. Defensively, she answered, "Well, it can't all be a lie."

Roman sighed and sat back, staring at the ceiling. "Aren't you supposed to be telling me about Anika?"

"It's equally important that we know about you and what kind of situation Annie would be going into."

"Since when is it the job of a volunteer art teacher to make decisions on child placement?"

Paige's mouth opened, then closed before her indignation could form into words. He was right, it was not her job. "I'm sorry. It's just that. . .I want what's best for her. I want to see her raised in a good Chris—"

Roman gave a wicked laugh. "Miss Stern, I was raised in a 'good Christian home'! I had the fear of God shoved down my throat before I was weaned! I learned the Ten Commandments backwards, forwards, and inside-out, never had a TV, and didn't wear jeans 'til I was eighteen. When I was twelve years old my father made me copy the entire Gospel of John as punishment for going to see a Muppet movie with a friend. You have before you a true product of Hell-fire and brimstone! Like what you see, Miss Stern?"

"But that's—"

"That's Christianity, Miss Stern!"

"No, it's not! It's a distortion of the truth. If you'd listened to the Book of John while you were copying it, you'd know those things have nothing to do with the character of Christ!"

"Don't start the God-is-love stuff on me."

"But He is love! Jesus came to set us free! That kind of teaching just puts chains on people; it keeps you from knowing the grace and mercy of God, it steals the joy and the peace!"

He sneered at her. "You're a great example of peace

and joy, Miss Stern! If I want preaching I'll go home to my father. I came here to find out about my daughter."

Paige froze, then took a deep breath and let it out slowly. "Ever hear of the group Petra?"

"Yeah."

"They have a song that says, 'Sometimes God's children should be seen and not heard.' I guess this was one of those times."

Quietly, she began to tell him about Annie, her routine, her favorite foods and toys, and how to handle her tantrums. That was the point that brought tears to her eyes. "The strangest things can set her off. Usually it's not getting her way, but sometimes it's something completely unpredictable. One day I wore a yellow blouse; it's not a color I usually wear, maybe that was it, but she wouldn't come near me, she just started screaming and throwing blocks."

"And all you have to do when she gets like that is hold her down until she stops, right?"

Paige took another deep breath. This man was not father material. "You hold her, not hold her down. She needs to feel safe, that she has boundaries."

Maybe it was her tears, but something seemed to soften Roman. The defiance seemed to ebb away into a kind of tired frustration. Shaking his head, Roman said, "I have no experience in this area. I'll have to hire live-in help for awhile and find a specialist in FAS."

"Why are you doing this, Mr. Slayder? Why do you want her?"

"She's my daughter."

"Is it a guilt thing? I don't mean to sound harsh, but is it just a matter of feeling responsible for her? Because if that's what it is maybe it would help you to know that there's another. . .party. . .interested in adopting her."

"Dr. Worth never mentioned that."

"No. . .I don't suppose he would."

Roman walked toward the leather chair across from her. Slowly he sat down, staring at her for a full minute before speaking. "I've made some big mistakes in my life. Anika is the result of one of them, and there are other consequences to the kind of life I've lived." He paused and searched her face. "Can I trust you not to repeat this?" Paige nodded and he said, "Due to. . .let's just say medical reasons. . .Anika is the only child I will ever father. I'm in a serious relationship with a very giving woman who was thrilled to find out I have a child. I may not be your idea of a father, but I want to make this work."

Paige swiped at a stray tear. "I understand," she said.

He leaned toward her. "You're the 'other party,' aren't you? The one who was interested in adopting Anika."

"Yes."

"I'm sorry things aren't working out the way you'd hoped."

Paige sighed. "And I'm sorry I came on so strong. I'm sure it would be best for Annie to be with her own father."

Fingering the silver medallion, Roman said, "Don't apologize; you've said some things tonight that I need to think about. The only thing I'm sure of about parenting is that I don't want to be like my father. I turned my back on God because of him—but maybe I never knew God because of him."

thirteen

Brant was sound asleep when Paige walked into the break room. She fought the desire to kiss him on the forehead to wake him, marveling that the idea seemed so natural. Instead, she whispered his name and he opened one eye.

"How'd it go?" he asked, his voice thick from sleep. "I've been praying for you."

She smiled at him. "It looks like it." She watched as he sat up and ran his hand across his face, then reached down for his boots. "How long has it been since you've had a full night's sleep?"

Brant yawned. "About three weeks, I guess. I haven't had a full day off since I started. I need the overtime. But I'm not scheduled to work tomorrow. How about you?"

"I'm off. I did the scheduling this week, so that's one of the perks."

"Good." Brant put his boots on and stood up. "So how did it go with Roman?"

"Not great. I wasn't exactly salt and light."

"It's hard to let go and let God be God sometimes, isn't it?"

"I guess that's what's at the heart of it, isn't it?—wanting my own way."

"That's what's at the heart of all our problems." Brant followed Paige out the back door to the parking lot. As they walked to her car, he looked up. The sky was velvet-black and sprayed with stars. "Would have been a perfect night for a flight." As he opened her car door he asked, "Do you have plans for tomorrow?"

"No." When he got in on the passenger side, he asked, "Sure you're serious about flying lessons?"

"Yes. . .serious, but a little scared."

"That's normal."

Paige fastened her seat belt and started the car. She was pulling out onto the road before she said, "I had a friend from here who died on his first solo flight in a Cessna. Did you know Gavin Prentice?"

"Yeah, I knew him. He was high before he ever got up in the air; he shouldn't have been flying."

The tone in his voice told her the topic was closed. It wasn't hard to understand. She changed the subject. "So you grew up in Milbrooke?"

"Off and on."

She glanced at him, then back at the road. "I don't think I understand."

"Neither did I," he said ruefully. Pointing to the left when she came to a stop sign, he said, "My parents are photo-journalists. They did assignments for *National Geographic* and several book publishers. They were gone more than they were home. Once in a great while we'd travel with them; we spent one summer in Peru, actually living in the same apartment, but my sister and I were basically raised by our grandparents."

"That must have been hard." She paused a minute. "Is that why you're so against me adopting Annie?"

"Yes and no. I have some pretty intense feelings about parents taking responsibility for their own kids, but in this case I'm not sure Roman is the best one to care for Annie."

"But you're not sure that I am either."

Brant pointed to the gravel drive leading to his house and turned to face her. "I think you have all the qualities of an excellent mother."

Paige pulled the car to a stop in front of a small white frame house. "Are you noticing a pattern here? Why is it that as soon as this subject comes up we're out of time?"

Brant laughed and looked at the digital clock. It read 11:26. "Who says we're out of time? We're off tomorrow. You hungry? I can throw a pizza in the oven."

"Sounds good. Come to think of it, I haven't eaten since noon."

As Brant opened the side door to the house he said, "I'm warning you—think bachelor!"

The warning was well-founded. As Paige walked up the three steps to the kitchen, she tripped over a pair of running shoes with socks hanging out of them.

"Sorry," Brant said, catching her by the arm. "Here, stand here and don't move." Paige obeyed and laughed as she watched him fly through the room, scooping up dirty dishes and papers from the counter and table. When he started taking notes and lists off the refrigerator, she said, "Stop! All you have to do is clear a path! I live with a girl who's never made a bed in her life—I'll feel out of place if it's too clean!"

Looking slightly embarrassed, Brant swept the room with his eyes and, piling a stack of papers on top of the refrigerator, pronounced it passable. Paige walked around the small, linoleum-floored room. Except for the microwave and the cordless phone sitting on the counter, the kitchen could have been a page out of a *Better Homes and*

Gardens from the fifties. A gray Formica-topped table with four chrome chairs sat in front of a bay window. Next to the white porcelain sink was a pink stove and a matching refrigerator stood next to the window. Paige touched the pink dotted-swiss curtains. The material was so faded and thin she was afraid her touch would pull them down.

"Quite a museum, huh?" Brant said, opening the freezer compartment on the refrigerator. "My grandparents were not the progressive type. Believe me, I've got plans."

Paige touched the once-white plastic shade on the light fixture that hung low over the table. "I love this!"

Turning from the oven, Brant arched one eyebrow and laughed. "I thought you were an artist!"

"This is so. . .authentic; it's so old it's in! You should leave it just the way it is!"

Brant shook his head. "Clear a place and sit down." Lifting a Bible and a copy of *My Utmost for His Highest* off a plastic-cushioned chair, Paige asked, "How long have you been a Christian?"

He turned to face the counter. "Only about five years."

She stared at his back, waiting for him to say more. "Go on. Did Cody lead you to the Lord?"

Brant took the wrapper off the frozen pizza. "He had a lot to do with it."

"Go on."

"Cody and I have been friends since junior high; we got in a lot of trouble together in high school. He accepted the Lord when we were sixteen. I thought he was nuts, but I guess I had the attitude that everybody's got to do his own thing. We stayed friends even though we didn't have a lot in common anymore. After high school we got together when we were both home on vacations. He kept talking about God and I kept ignoring him."

He was quiet for a long time, and then he turned slowly, crossing his arms over his chest and leaning back against the counter. He stared at her, opened his mouth, then closed it as if changing his mind about what he was going to say. After a few more seconds he said, "Then I got into a relationship with a Christian girl and I guess the timing was right, 'cause I was finally ready to listen. God was so real to her. . ."

Brant's eyes locked with hers and Paige felt the same discomfort she had felt at the restaurant. "She loved Jesus with every ounce of her being. She taught me the meaning of dying to self, of total surrender to God's will. . ."

Paige shifted in her chair and looked away from him. She was ashamed to admit to herself that what she was feeling was envy, not just because of the glowing admiration he had for this girl, but because there had been a time in her life when people could have said the same things about her. "Do you still. . .see her?"

Brant smiled wistfully. "Yeah. But things are different between us now."

"But you still care about her?"

He shrugged. "I owe her a lot. I hope I can tell her that someday."

He opened the oven door and slid the pizza onto the rack. "So what's your story?"

"I was raised in a Christian home, went to Christian schools, camps, retreats. . .you name it, but I went through a weird phase right after high school. I joined an artist's colony for two years and tried on a lot of different philosophies. When I got tired of starving and being around really strange people, I went to college. It was a secular school, but a huge revival hit the campus in my senior year. We had all-night prayer meetings, hundreds of kids accepted Christ. . .it was so awesome. That's when I finally understood that kind of complete surrender you were talking about. A bunch of us were reading a book about the early Christians, and I remember feeling like a kindred spirit with them. Back then I knew that I could be mauled by lions or burned at the stake and never deny Christ. I knew His grace was sufficient and nothing else mattered."

Again, she looked away from him, feeling too vulnerable beneath his searching eyes. "Before the sun comes up I really do want to hear your opinion about Annie."

"So you think!"

"Well, things look different now. Since there isn't much chance it's actually going to happen, I think I can handle it with a little less emotion."

Brant set the timer on the stove and sat down across from her. "This is going to sound presumptuous coming from someone you just met." He leaned toward her, and once again Paige had the feeling she was an open book and he was turning the pages. "I think your motives are wrong," he said. "Adoption is a beautiful thing, but I think you're looking at this for selfish reasons. I think you're looking for an easy way to fill a void."

Paige drew back as if he'd slapped her. "There's nothing easy about taking care of a child like Annie!"

"True. But maybe in your mind it's less threatening than the real answer." He reached out and touched her arm. "Paige, let go of your pride long enough to ask yourself if it's the truth."

fourteen

Watching the red glow of Paige's tail lights fade into the blackness, Brant ran his hand through his hair and sighed. "You're crossing the line," he said to himself out loud. He'd made a promise to himself the day Cody introduced him to Paige, a promise that he would keep his distance from her, both physically and emotionally. And just an hour ago, with his hand on her arm and his eyes locked on hers, he'd broken it. Not only was his hand touching her arm, but he could feel his heart reaching out to her. He shook his head in disgust at himself.

Back inside, he threw away the paper plates and soda cans and took the pile of papers down from the top of the refrigerator and set it on the table. He put the notes and lists back under the magnets on the refrigerator door and set his flight log back on the counter next to the phone, then picked up his Bible and the Oswald Chambers book that Paige had been looking at.

He opened the devotional book. Halfway down the page he read, "To be a disciple is to be a devoted love-slave of the Lord Jesus. Many of us who call ourselves Christians are not devoted to Jesus Christ." He finished reading the passage and turned to a page that he had highlighted in blue. There he read about being broken bread and poured-out wine, about being nourishment for others until they learned to feed on God.

Closing the book, he turned off the lights and headed for the bedroom. Sitting down on the chenille spread, he turned on the lamp on the bedside table and kicked off his boots. He pulled his shirt off and lay down, still in his jeans and wool socks. A slight breeze was fluttering the curtains and making the lilac branches tap against the window. Brant closed his eyes, but knew that, as tired as he was, sleep would not come easily. His mind was heavy with thoughts of a girl whose words had changed his life.

Was he setting himself up for disappointment by hoping for that kind of oneness again? And what made him think that this woman with the red nails and the hair that fell over one side of her face was even capable of the kind of depth he was searching for? He rolled toward the wall, staring at the magnolia blossoms on the peeling gray wallpaper, trying not to see her face. He'd seen something break in her when he told her to let go of her pride, and the feeling it sent through him had shaken his very being. It was all he could do not to take her in his arms. But he had no right to do that. Any affection he showed her now could, in the long run, just cause them both pain.

Was he wrong to commit himself to helping her figure out what he already knew about her? Was he capable of denying his own emotions for the sake of opening her eyes to the truth? Truth—did he even have the right to use the word? Brant sat up and cradled his face in his hands. "Lord, let me be broken bread and poured-out wine for You, for her. Help me draw her back to You. But if You ask me to walk out of her life, I will."

Still in his jeans, he turned off the light, wrapped the spread around himself, and continued to pray until a pale amber light filtered through the holes in the curtains and he fell asleep.

❧

Paige tip-toed up the carpeted stairs, carrying her heels in one hand. But in spite of her quiet, the lamp in Hailey's room came on when she got to the landing and Hailey called to her. Paige dropped her shoes in the hallway and walked into the room, taking off her earrings as she walked.

Hailey sat up in bed. "Were you talking to Roman this whole time?"

"No."

"Where were you?"

"Well, Mom, if you must know, I was with Brant."

"Oooo! Tell me everything!"

Unbuckling her belt, Paige said, "After I get out of this."

She walked into her room pulling her dress over her head. Opening her top drawer, she tossed her earrings into an open box, but one bounced out and fell onto a stack of books on the floor. Sitting on top was a copy of *The Velveteen Rabbit.* Of all the books in her collection, this was by far her favorite. She had sent a copy to Gavin, the only gift she had ever sent him. In it she had written, "Sometimes it hurts when God makes us real, but it's worth the pain."

She put the earring away, slipped into her nightgown, and went back to Hailey's room. As she flopped down on the bed, Hailey said, "Well?"

Paige threw up her hands. "The man has me completely confused."

With a sarcastic smile and a voice to match, Hailey said, "Poor baby. You've never been confused by a man before, have you?"

Paige picked up a heart-shaped lace pillow and threw it

at her. "Do you want to hear this or not?"

Leaning forward, Hailey brushed her hand across her face in an attempt to wipe away the smile. "Okay, I'm serious now. But it's true—this is different for you, isn't it? He's not like most of the guys that trail after you." Quickly holding up her hand, she said, "Sorry, that just slipped out!"

"He's not like any guy I've ever met anywhere! Is that a cliché line or what? But it's true! A week ago I had him pegged for an egotistical jerk, and now I'm seeing this whole other side. He's strong—emotionally, spiritually—"

"And physically!"

"Like I need you to point that out, girl! Help me stay a little objective here, please!"

"Sorry—again. Let's concentrate on character. He has a soft side. Cody told me about a time he ran into a deer with his car and cried like a baby."

Paige blinked her eyes and wiped away imaginary tears. "See? That's what's so confusing about him! He's not afraid to say what he thinks, to the point of almost being cruel . . .but he's not. But there's this gentleness in him, too. And his faith is so real, so. . .'intense' is the only word I can think of. The way he prays. . .he knows God. And he knows other things. Have you been talking to him about me?"

"No, but Cody has."

"I guess that would explain it. What did they talk about?"

"What's it worth to you?"

"Dishes for a week."

"Keep going."

"I promise not to put Limburger cheese on your engine after your wedding."

"You're good, you know."

"I know. Talk."

"This comes from the analytical mind of a lawyer, remember. Cody said that if you just listened to Brant's words you'd think he wasn't the least bit interested, but if you read between the lines you can see that he's fighting some sort of pretty strong feelings about you. He keeps saying that you're not his type, but Cody keeps telling him that there's more to you than satin and pearls!"

Paige sat up. "Is that how he sees me?"

"It's all talk. Cody says it won't take much at all for you to have him wrapped around your little finger if you want."

"I don't want!" Paige pounded her fist on the bed. "That's the last thing in the world I want! And I think Cody's got him figured all wrong—I think Brant McCourt is one of the few men on earth that no woman could wrap around her finger!"

With a knowing smile, Hailey leaned forward and whispered, "And that's exactly what you like about him."

∾

Since Brant's truck was already at the airport, Paige had agreed to pick him up at two. When she got to his house, he was sitting on the front step with the cordless phone in his hand. He motioned for her to join him.

"Hi! You look nice, not like a woman who was out partying until two in the morning. Did you sleep late?"

She couldn't tell him that she'd spent half of what was left of the night talking to Hailey about him and that the rest of the early morning hours were spent tossing and turning and thinking about him. "Not too late," she answered honestly. "How about you?"

He wouldn't tell her he'd spent the night wrestling with his pillow and his memories and counting magnolias in the moonlight. He wouldn't tell her he'd prayed for her until the sun came up. "Slept enough, I guess," he said. "I'm trying to call for a weather briefing. The line was busy." He pushed the redial button and waited, then said, "Good morning. I'd like a standard weather briefing for a VFR flight from Milbrooke, C48, to Oshkosh, OSH. The aircraft is a Cessna 150, 714 Echo Tango. Departure time 2:30 local. Altitude 3,000 feet." Listening to the response, he nodded. "Thank you. Have a nice day."

Turning to her he said, "Sounds like a beautiful day to fly. There's some rain predicted for the northeast part of the state, but it should be too far north to bother us. There's a light wind, but it should be a pretty smooth flight. I'll go grab a couple jackets."

Paige walked to the car, staring up at the cloudless sky. A surge of excitement coursed through her as she realized that in less than an hour she would be up there. As Brant joined her in the car, she asked, "How long have you been flying?"

"About nine years. I got my license just before my twenty-first birthday. It was something I'd wanted to do since I was a little kid. I was going to EMT school at the same time, but I didn't have any thoughts of putting them together and making a career out of it until a couple years later. In the beginning, I just loved the feeling, the freedom. You really get a perspective of how insignificant we are from up there. Houses and cars shrink into these little Monopoly tokens, and fields and roads turn into squares in a patchwork quilt. . ."

Paige looked at him and smiled. "That's very poetic."

"Does that surprise you?"

"Yes. You don't seem like the poetic type to me."

"But you like surprises, remember."

She gave him a sideways look, wondering again how he knew that. "Have you ever had an accident? A crash landing or anything?"

"Never. A couple scares, but nothing more. Any landing you walk away from is a good one!" He grinned and watched the reaction on her face. "Flying a plane is safer than driving a car. Even if we lose an engine we can still land the plane!"

Brant walked up to the desk in the small office and said, "How's it going, Kip? Would you hand me the log book and the key for *Echo Tango*?"

"Where you headed?"

"Just around here for a short lesson first." He introduced Paige to the man behind the counter. "Then we'll take off to Oshkosh for dinner."

Kip arched his eyebrows and eyed Paige, who was looking at the aerial view pictures on the wall. "I see. . . like you do with all your first time students."

Brant smiled, even while he managed to silence Kip with a warning look, took the three-ring notebook, and opened the door for Paige.

The top half of the two-passenger Cessna was white and the bottom half was bright red. "Looks like someone dipped it in catsup," Paige said.

Brant shook his head. "You sound like someone who should be illustrating children's books instead of painting portraits." He opened the pilot side door for her. Paige looked inside, then back at him.

"Aren't I supposed to get in the other side?" she asked nervously.

"This is 'hands on' learning." He looked down at her,

noticing for the first time the large gold barrette holding her hair away from her face. Tapping it with his finger, he said, "Smart." When she still hadn't made a move to get in the plane, he took her chin gently in his hand and turned her face toward the passenger side. "Look in there. I have identical controls. I'll handle the take-off and the landing and I'll talk you through every step in between. When your yoke moves, so does mine, and I can take over any time I need to."

He turned her back to face him, lifting her chin just slightly. "Trust me," he whispered.

Paige felt her knees grow weak and told herself it was just nerves. She had to turn away from him and the only way to get away from him was to get in the plane.

Brant walked around to the other side. Detaching the key from one of the rings inside the log book, he handed it to her. "Okay," he said, "find the ignition switch down on the left hand side; put the key in but don't turn it. Now, see the red flag behind the yoke that says 'control wheel lock'? Pull that straight up, it'll slide out, then reach around and put it in the pocket behind your seat. Now, see the switch right next to the ignition switch? It says 'master switch.' Switch that on. Over here is the flap control switch, slide it down to ten degrees. Turn the master switch off again and check down on the floor in the middle and make sure that the fuel shut-off valve points to 'on.' Now, get back out of the plane and we'll do the rest of our inspection outside."

Paige waited for him on her side of the plane. When he reached her, she said, "Aren't I supposed to take driver's ed. or flight simulation or something first?"

Putting his hands on her shoulders, he said in a mad

scientist voice, "Trust me, my dear, I know what I'm doing."

They walked around the plane counter-clockwise, going over each step on the pre-flight checklist, examining all moveable parts, the inflation of the tires, the oil and fuel levels. Then he led her back to the pilot's side and motioned for her to get in. Bending over to show her how to adjust her seat belt, he leaned close to her ear, close enough that she could feel the warmth of his breath against her cheek. "Trust me?" he asked.

Numbly, Paige nodded, grateful she didn't have to walk with her legs turning to jelly. All she had to do was fly a plane. With her hands and feet resting lightly on the yoke and rudder controls, she listened as Brant explained every move he made. As he started the engine and began taxiing down the runway, he picked up the radio microphone and said, "Milbrooke traffic, this is 7-1-4 *Echo Tango* departing runway two niner."

To Paige he said, "You shove the throttle lever all the way in. Watch the air speed indicator. When we reach 55 knots, we're going to lift off the runway by gently pulling back on the yoke. Just feel the movement of the yoke. We'll keep the air speed at about 60 to 65 knots as we climb." He glanced at her face as the wheels left the runway and saw the look of wonder he was hoping to find. "When we reach 1,400 feet, that's about 500 feet off the ground, we're going to make a gentle turn to the north as we continue to climb."

As they leveled off at 3,000 feet above sea level, Paige looked down for the first time and felt her anxiety level begin to lower. *Brant was right,* she thought, *there is freedom up here.*

"Okay, Amelia Erhart," he said, "it's your turn now. I'll

talk you through it. I want you to gently pull back on the yoke until the nose of the plane lifts a little. You'll feel a little forward pressure, but just try to hold the yoke steady. Good. You're doing great. Now turn just a little to the right and keep holding a little backward pressure on the yoke."

He guided her in a wide circle, pointing out the Sparrow Center and, a few minutes later, David and Karlee's house. "I don't know where you live," he said, "think you can find it?"

"It's about two miles south of—"

A sudden bump rocked the plane. Paige gripped the yoke. "What did we hit?"

Brant turned to smile at her. "There's not much to run into up here."

"But—"

Suddenly, the aircraft jumped and Paige felt like she was in free-fall for a split second. Instinctively she pulled back on the yoke, causing the plane to climb sharply. Brant pressed his yoke forward, counteracting her move. "Let go, Paige, let me have it."

When his words pierced her moment of panic, she relaxed her hold and he leveled the plane off. "It's all yours again," he said, with no hint of criticism.

"I overreacted, huh?"

Trying not to laugh, he said, "You could say that. A little more to the right."

"It was just turbulence, right?"

"Right."

A few minutes went by and then Paige said, "That wasn't so bad. I'll get the hang of this."

Sliding his left hand over her right, Brant said, "You're gonna do just fine."

fifteen

When they landed at the Oshkosh airport, Brant reached behind the seat and handed her a leather aviator's jacket. "Here, you might need this. Besides, it makes you look the part."

He had called a taxi before they left Milbrooke and it took them to a restaurant overlooking Lake Winnebago, where Brant had reserved a table on the deck. The late afternoon sun sparkled on the water and the wind feathered the fringe on the umbrella above them. Paige gave the waitress her order, then pulled a pen out of her pocket and began drawing on her napkin. Brant watched in silent interest.

When she finished, she handed him the cartoon that depicted him landing a plane in a pool of catsup. He laughed and tucked it in his pocket as the waitress brought their drinks. "That's your real gift, you know."

Quietly, she said, "Yeah, maybe some day. . ." then sat back and took a sip of the virgin Pina Colada that had been served her in a coconut shell. Lifting an aristocratic little finger, she said, "Well, daahling, shall we do breakfast in New York and then dinner in Miami?"

"Sounds delightful, my dear. I take it you're growing fond of this lifestyle—in spite of a little turbulence?"

"There is turbulence in every lifestyle, sir. One must learn to take the bad with the good."

"Well said, ma'am. And does one take one's own advice frequently?"

"Never!" Paige laughed and bent to take another sip from her straw.

Somewhere between here and the airport, he noticed, she had removed the barrette and her hair spilled over her cheek again. He reached across the table and tucked it behind her ear. "I've wanted to do that for a long time," he said.

Cocking her head to the side so that several strands of hair escaped, she smiled coyly. "Why?"

Reaching out and repeating the gesture, he said, "Because I feel like you're hiding from me."

"I thought men liked a little mystery in women."

"A little, yes. Too much makes a man wonder if he's being pushed away."

He was staring through her again, but this time she didn't look away. He'd made a statement, but it was really a question. "I'm not pushing you away."

She expected him to take her hand then, but instead he sat back in his chair and said, "So how are wedding plans coming on the bride's side? The groom is counting the hours and becoming a real pain to be around."

"As of four o'clock this morning everything was running smoothly, but that was twelve hours ago. Every once in a while I hear her gasp and start talking to herself about something she forgot. I can't imagine what she'd be like if they were planning a big wedding! Actually, for once I've been really grateful for her incessant chatter."

"Keeps your mind off things?"

"Mmm-hm."

"When will you hear about Annie?"

"They'll be starting the home study on Roman soon, then it'll be a few weeks before they make a decision."

"That could get nerve-wracking."

"You're being very understanding for someone who thinks I'm totally off base!"

"All the more reason for me to be concerned!"

"Well, for right now you don't have to worry about me flipping out or anything. After the wedding, who knows . . .I may hijack a plane and fly Annie to Tahiti!"

Brant laughed. "Don't take this personally, but I don't think you'll be quite ready to cross any borders by yourself in two weeks!"

"Fine. Then I'll hijack you, too."

"I could handle that."

The waitress brought a plate of relishes and a bread basket. Paige chewed on a carrot, thinking. Suddenly she said, "Could this just be a test? Like Abraham and Isaac, you know? Is God just waiting for me to give up and then He'll let me have her?"

Cautiously, Brant said, "It could be. Or it could be just like you said—that this isn't about you or Annie, it's about Roman."

"But why would God want her raised by a heathen father instead of a Christian mother?"

The look Brant returned was the look her father used to give her just before grounding her to her room. *He may have a soft side,* she thought, *but the egotism is still alive and well.* "You don't approve of my question?"

"Do you really want to get into this here and now?" he asked. "If this is all we ever talk about I don't think we'll ever get beyond potential friends. By the way, how close are we getting to being real friends?"

"I'll let you know after you say what you're thinking."

"You're a glutton for punishment, aren't you? Keep in mind that you asked for this. . ." He took a deep breath and stared out at the lake, then turned back to face her, leaning his chin on his folded hands. "Humor me for a minute here—I'm going to try to make this an object lesson. Before we hit that turbulence this afternoon, who was in control?"

"I was. . .well, sort of."

"What would have happened if you had ignored me or fought me when I told you to let go of the yoke?"

"I don't know, but it wouldn't have been good."

"We would have continued climbing until the engine stalled and we dropped like a rock."

"I think I don't like what you're implying. . ."

"Don't get defensive on me. This isn't an attack."

"I know, but it's starting to feel uncomfortable."

"Hebrews 10:24 says, 'And let us consider how we may spur one another on toward love and good deeds.' I'm just spurring."

"Spurs hurt."

"So does the truth sometimes."

"Okay, go on. Spur away."

"Remember that bumper sticker that said, 'God is my co-pilot'?"

"Yes. I'm going to take some real offense here if you're saying God is not my co-pilot. In the first place. . ."

"Hold on a minute! If you're going to get mad, wait for what I'm going to say next! There was another bumper sticker that came out after that one had been around for awhile. It said, 'If God is your co-pilot, you're in the wrong seat!'"

The waitress brought their food then. After Brant prayed, Paige turned her attention to her plate of shrimp scampi, but her mind was on Brant's words. After several minutes she said, "To use your own words, 'this is going to sound presumptuous coming from someone you don't know very well,' but I think that you and I may be guilty of the same problem." She answered the question on Brant's face. "Hailey accused me of comparing every guy I meet to Gavin. I gather that you didn't like him, but I think I knew a side of him that very few people saw. Still, it's been five years and time turns people into legends. You know what I mean?"

Brant nodded slowly, looking uncomfortable. It was obvious to Paige that he had expected to stay in control of the conversation. "That girl you told me about, the one that led you to the Lord? . . . Are you sure you're not doing the same with her? The same thing I've been doing with Gavin, expecting everyone to live up to a standard that's not realistic. And passing judgment when they don't." She met his eyes squarely. "I'm not that girl, Brant. I'm quieter about my faith, more private; not everyone runs around saying 'praise the Lord' and 'Hallelujah' every other word! I don't think you've known me long enough to make a judgment on where I'm at with God. And I don't know why you feel compelled to steer every single conversation around to my relationship with the Lord!" Jabbing a piece of shrimp with her fork, Paige felt her face color. Not only was she being defensive, she realized, she was also telling him loud and clear that she was jealous of this saintly legend from his past.

"Paige, I have no desire to fight with you, but you did ask for my opinion."

"About Annie!"

"It's all the same subject. Adopting her would be a kind, generous, noble thing to do, but is it what God wants for your life? Are you listening to Him? Please don't take this as an attack; this is something I challenge myself with every day. Am I completely surrendered? Am I truly dead to self and being clay in the potter's hands? And I think we're supposed to challenge each other that way, don't you? I don't think that's being judgmental. Christ is the standard we're all trying to live up to, not any person. Right?"

"Yes. . .of course." Paige squirmed in her seat, trying to think of the words that would explain her discomfort. "But—but, do you do this with everyone you meet? Don't you have to get to know someone before you start pointing out their weak points?"

Brant pushed his half-finished plate aside and reached for her hand. He ran his fingertip around the pearl on her ring. "I know it doesn't make sense, but I feel like I do know you, and I have this strong feeling that you're going through the motions of faith, but you're afraid to let go of the yoke."

Laying down her fork, Paige moved her drink closer and began stirring it with the straw, watching it swirl like a miniature cyclone.

"Say something," Brant said.

She looked up at him with a weak smile. "Ouch," she said.

sixteen

On the day of Hailey's wedding, Paige was smiling to herself as she walked down the stairs. At the bottom of the steps she stopped and picked up the camera that hung from her neck. Before her, in the living room, was a picture worth saving. Karlee, in a dress that looked like the field of wildflowers next to the house, was sitting in a rocking chair next to the stone fireplace nursing Jordan. The afternoon sun glinted on the diamond in the gold cross necklace that hung down next to Jordan's tiny fist. While Karlee's left hand supported the baby, the other combed her daughter's satiny blond hair.

Shelly, kneeling on the braided rug in a dress that matched her mother's, looked up when the camera flashed and grinned at Paige. Smiling back at Shelly, Paige said, "You're getting to be a regular pro at this flower girl stuff, aren't you Princess?"

Shelly nodded. "Aunt Hailey says I get to be in your wedding next."

"Oh, does she? And I suppose Aunt Hailey has decided who I'm going to marry?"

"Uh-huh. Even I know that! Brant is sooo cute!"

Karlee laughed. "Out of the mouths of babes. . ."

"Has he kissed you yet?" Shelly asked.

Karlee's jaw dropped. "Shelly! That's rude!" But over the top of the little blond head she mouthed, "Well?"

"No, he has not kissed me. We haven't even gone out. . . exactly. We're just friends."

"Uh-huh," mother and daughter said in unison.

The sound of the back door opening saved Paige from further questioning. Ruth Austin, Karlee and Hailey's mother, walked into the room. "Oh, look at you girls!" she exclaimed. "You all look so pretty!" She walked over to Shelly and hugged her, then touched the top of Jordan's head. "If you need someone to burp him when he's done. . ." she offered. Turning to Paige she said, "I think my girls will be happy to see me leave. I'm supposed to be here helping Karlee with the house and Hailey with the wedding, but I've spent most of the time holding this baby!"

"That's what Grammas are for," Paige said, while motioning for her to stand behind Karlee for a three generation picture.

"Where's David?" Karlee asked her mother.

"He and Dad and T.J. are all dressed and headed over to, as T.J. put it, 'make Cody a nervous wreck.' They dropped me off in the driveway and said they weren't stepping one foot inside a house full of primping women!"

"We've taught them well," Karlee said. Ruth nodded. "How's Hailey doing?"

Paige laughed. "She's upstairs babbling to herself about how happy she is that they decided on a small outdoor wedding without a ton of attendants and hundreds of guests because there's no pressure and it doesn't even matter if it starts raining because they can just wait for the rain to stop because they haven't rented a hall and it doesn't matter what time the reception starts and everything is just so low-key that she's not even the least bit nervous!"

"In other words, my little girl's a basket case!"

"You got it."

With a deep breath, Ruth turned toward the stairs.

"Wait, Mom," Karlee called to her. Reaching down, she picked up a small jewelry box and handed it to her mother. "You should be the one to give it to her." Taking it from her, Ruth blinked back the tears that filled her eyes. Karlee smiled. "Don't fight it, Mom. Just have a good cry and get it out of your system so you can touch up your mascara before the wedding."

Pulling a tissue out of her pocket, Ruth said, "We've just been so lucky. . .no, we've been so blessed—you girls have taught me that. Seeing both of you so happy, and a new grandchild, and Dad feeling better than he had for years before his stroke. . .I guess I have every right to a few tears!" With that, she headed up the stairs.

Several minutes later she came back down, still in tears, leading the way for Hailey. As Hailey descended the open staircase, Shelly let out a long "Oooo!" that was echoed by Paige and Karlee. The fringe from the soft buckskin dress flared out from her sleeves and hem as she twirled before her audience. Her dark auburn hair fell in loose curls to her waist; the blue of her eyes was echoed in the beaded band across her forehead and the polished stones in her copper earrings. From a fine gold chain around her neck hung the teardrop pearl that had been worn by her grandmother, her mother, and twice by Karlee.

Shelly stepped closer and reached out to touch Hailey's sleeve. "You're beautiful," she whispered. "Something old is your dress, something borrowed is Mama's sandals, and you have lots of something blue, but what's your something new?"

"I just got it last night," Hailey said. Pulling her sleeve back, she showed them the braided copper bracelet on her wrist

"Did Cody give it to you?" Shelly asked dreamily.

"No. I got this from. . ." She stopped, determined not to cry. "I got this from Cody's birth father."

≈

The little stone church had guarded the river bank for more than ninety years. A cobblestone walkway curved from the heavy oak door on it's south side to the arched footbridge that connected the church yard with the cemetery. Pink and white impatiens and purple alyssum ran along both sides of the path. Today, five people stood in the mid-day sunlight at the foot of the bridge as guitar music drifted out over the river.

Karlee, standing next to Hailey, smiled at David, who sat in the front row of folding chairs holding Jordan. Then she turned her eyes to the church door where her oldest son stood, straight as a soldier, holding the ring pillow. Finally, she looked at Shelly, her hair shining in the sunlight as she walked toward Cody and Hailey, scattering rose petals from the basket on her arm. Karlee pulled a tissue from beneath her bouquet and wiped her eyes.

Crouching on the grass in a dress of unbleached muslin, Paige focused the camera on Cody's face as he lifted Hailey's hand in his and began to recite the vows he had written. "A cord of three strands is not quickly broken. As you and I come together before our Lord, we will draw our strength from him and we will strengthen each other. You are my best friend, Hailey; your love and your trust are precious gifts. . ." He stopped to steady his voice, and Paige lifted the camera again, but found it hard to clear her eyes long enough to focus.

Giving up, she went back to her chair next to David. She listened to Cody's words, and then Hailey's, followed by the traditional vows, but she found her eyes drawn to Brant. Like Cody, he wore black jeans and a silk shirt with a bolo tie. Cody's shirt was off-white, while Brant's was a bright blue. Even from where she sat, she could see what the color did to his eyes.

After the exchange of rings, Cody and Hailey stood facing each other, holding hands. With his cane in one hand and his guitar slung over his shoulder, Richard Wingreen, Cody's birth father, walked behind them to the top of the bridge and began to sing. The sound of the river backdropped his words: ". . .and I don't even know her name, but I'm praying for her just the same, that the Lord will write His name upon her heart. Cause somewhere in the course of his life, my little boy will need a Godly wife, so hold on to Jesus, baby, wherever you are. . ." The words sent a shiver down Paige's spine.

During a lull between hugging and tears and pictures, Paige walked to the edge of the water and stood quietly observing. Annie, in the pink dress Paige had bought for her, was running behind Shelly like a baby duckling, never letting the older girl out of her sight. Little Jordan was being passed from lap to lap, with Gramma hovering close. Cody and Hailey stood between Robert and Richard with their arms around both of them. It was a scene that should have produced nothing but joy in Paige, but as she stood there by the water, other feelings were creeping in.

As if sensing her absence, Brant began looking around. He smiled when he saw her and came toward her. He was still ten feet away when he said, "You look beautiful."

When he reached her, he fingered the flowers embroidered on her bell sleeve. "I like this. You should be standing in my kitchen with this on. The time eras would just about match."

"I got it at a consignment shop in Boston called Trashcan Tessie's. It's a gen-u-ine hippie wedding dress; the original owner is now a grandmother. I thought it was fitting."

"It's perfect. So how's my potential friend doing today?"

"Feeling a little sorry for herself at the moment."

"That's understandable."

"You know what just hit me this week? Starting tonight, I'll be living alone for the first time in my life! I've traveled all over the world by myself, but I've always been going to someone."

"Want a little wisdom from someone older and wiser?"

"Speak, Oh Wise One!"

"When God puts us in a position of having to let go of something, He always replaces it—if we let Him. Sometimes we just need more of Him for awhile and sometimes He gives us a new mission. . .or a new friend."

Paige nodded. "That sounds like something I would have said a few years ago. Lately, every time something starts looking uncertain, I start scanning the horizon for the next job or adventure or relationship, always making sure I've got a safety net. I guess, in part, that's what Annie's been. Making plans for her kept me from thinking about being alone."

"You realize you're admitting I was right."

"Part right. I really do love her."

"I know."

"I keep thinking about what we talked about. Where

did I lose my first love? It happened so slowly; God kept getting edged out by all the attention I was giving my work and the excitement of Paris. Letting go again isn't going to be easy."

"No, it's not." Brant took her hand and headed toward the bridge. They stopped at the top and looked down at the water rushing beneath them. Lifting a piece of paint from the railing, Paige let it drop and watched it drift into the river.

"The scary thing is that I'm not sure I want to let go again."

Brant leaned on his elbows, his arm just barely touching hers. "I have a little sign on my dashboard that says 'Don't wait to want to'."

"You have an answer for everything, don't you?"

"Mmm-hm. Irritating, isn't it?"

"Yes! You're a walking book of proverbs! I feel like I'm hanging out with Solomon sometimes!"

Rubbing his chin and continuing to stare at the water, Brant said, "There are some striking similarities, aren't there?"

Before Paige could formulate a comeback, Shelly came running onto the bridge, towing Annie behind her. "Aunt Paige, Brant!" she called breathlessly. "They're going to cut the cake! You have to hurry, cause you have to take pictures! We have to have a picture cause Aunt Hailey promised she's going to smash cake all over Cody's face and in his hair and who knows what he's going to do her after that! Maybe they'll start a food fight and everybody will throw cake at everybody! Are you coming?"

"We're coming, Jabber Jaws!" Brant was shaking his head and laughing. Paige joined him.

"It's genetic," she said.

At the bottom of the bridge he took her hand and lifted it to his lips. "I want you to know that whenever being alone gets too much, you can call me. I'd leave my 700 wives and 300 concubines for you any day."

She squeezed his hand. "Thanks, Sol, you're a true friend."

seventeen

Lyn Casey looked at her watch as she left the break room to begin her third bed check of the night. It was 5:03 A.M. Shining her flashlight at the ceiling, she bent over the crib where fifteen-month-old Ryan lay sleeping peacefully. Pulling the blanket up to his chin, she said quietly, "Sleep tight, little one," and walked across the room to peek in the other crib.

In the next room, she reached over a bed rail to pull the covers away from the pillow. "You're going to get too hot like that, sweetheart," she whispered. She pulled the blanket back and gasped, then sighed in frustration at the empty bed. In her two months at the Sparrow Center, this was the third time this had happened. The first child had been found in the hallway asking for a drink; the second she had discovered sound asleep under his bed, so that was the first place she looked this time. Getting down on her knees and shining the flashlight along the floor, she quietly called, "Annie! Annie!"

She swept the light around the room, then opened the closet and looked behind the clothes. She checked the bathroom, then the resident's room across the hall. Zigzagging from room to room she checked every room in the east wing. Running down the hall, she tried the occupational therapy room and then the day room. Both were locked. Backtracking, she turned the corner and ran down

130

the hallway leading to the lobby, peering into the staff break room and every unlocked office on her way. When she reached the dimly lit lobby, she flipped the light switches and circled the room, searching behind every chair and calling Annie's name.

Running back to the nurse's station, she called breathlessly to the night supervisor. "I can't find Annie! Page Darla and Wendy—we have to check the west wing and the cafeteria and nursery. I've checked everything else! I'll start on the west wing."

She was already ten feet down the hall when the voice of the woman behind the desk stopped her. "Lyn, come here." Marie Wassal walked around to the other side of the counter. After thirty-one years of nursing, it took more than a misplaced child to alarm her. Placing both dark hands on the LPN's shoulders, she said, "Calm down, now start at the top."

"Annie's not in her bed, and I've looked all over and I can't find her!"

"Relax, Lyn, we'll find her. This happens. She was probably sleep walking and curled up in a corner somewhere. You check the rooms on the right, I'll do the left. Okay?"

Twenty minutes later, Lyn and three nurse's aides stood at the desk, staring at the head nurse. Marie threw up her hands. "This is ridiculous! What have we missed? We've covered every inch of this building and every outside door is locked. Lyn, you're sure she was there at three?"

"Yes! Her bunny had fallen on the floor and I picked it up and put it next to her and she hugged it in her sleep. Now the bunny's gone."

Without another word, Marie picked up the phone and dialed.

Robert answered the phone with his eyes still closed, but the panic in Marie's voice made him instantly alert. "Has anyone come or gone in the last few hours?"

"No."

"Anyone walk outside on break or run out to their car, anything that might have left the door unlocked even for a few minutes?"

"No. We've wracked our brains to think of any possibility. I've questioned the girls in the nursery and everyone on the floor. No one has left the building."

The red numbers on Robert's clock radio read 5:43. The shift would change in just over an hour. "All right. I'm on my way. I'm going to make a couple calls first. If I come up with anything, I'll call you right back." As he hung up the phone, he turned on the lamp and pulled a phone book out of the bedside table. After punching in the number and waiting, he listened with a sinking feeling to Paige's voice on the answering machine.

❧

At the end of his driveway, Robert turned left instead of right. There had been much controversy surrounding the Sparrow Center before they had even broken ground for the building, but so far they had disappointed their opposition by avoiding any hint of scandal. Annie's safety was more important than the reputation of the Center, but he was not about to report this until he had checked the most obvious possibilities.

A spray of gravel flew from beneath his tires as he turned into Paige's driveway. Jumping out, he ran to the garage and looked in the window, relieved to see her car still there. He knocked on first the back door and then the front, but she was obviously too sound asleep to hear. He walked back to the car and dialed David and Karlee's number. They would have a key to the house.

"David, we've got a. . .situation at the Center. I don't want to talk about it on the cell phone, but I need to talk to Paige right away. I'm at her house now; she hasn't answered the phone or the door, but her car is here so—"

"Is Hailey's Jeep there?"

"No."

There was a long pause on the other end. "A radiator hose broke in Paige's car on Thursday," David said finally. "She said she'd just use Hailey's until I had time to look at it."

This time it was Robert's turn for silence. He fought for a logical explanation. "Do you have any idea where she might be? Could she have gone to work early?"

"I doubt it, but I'll try calling. If she's not there, I'll try . . .she's been kind of strange lately. I'm worried about her."

"I think you'd better meet me at the Center, David."

Robert hung up and dialed the Sparrow Center. "I want you to call the police. And Marie—we need to keep this quiet. Please tell the staff not to talk to anyone but the authorities. Then call Nancy; tell her you can't explain over the phone, but ask her who she can get along without this morning. Then call those people and tell them they can have a few hours off with pay—tell them I've called a special third shift meeting or something. If any of your staff can stay for awhile it would be very helpful; they'll get time and a half. Let's try to have the smallest changeover possible. I'll be there in a few minutes."

A uniformed officer was standing at the nurse's station when Robert walked in, and another officer was walking down the hall toward Annie's room with Lyn. As Robert walked up to the desk, he heard the officer saying, "Mrs. Wassal, are you the only one answering the phone on third shift?"

"Yes."

"Have there been any disturbing calls during the night, anyone you didn't recognize?"

"No. There have been only two calls since midnight. The husband of one of the aides called about 2:30 and one of the LPNs that works in the nursery called in sick. That was all."

"Is there ever a time when no one is at the nurses' station?"

"Yes, not for very long, but there are many times that we're all busy with residents."

Robert held out his hand and introduced himself to the officer at the desk. Sergeant Jim Delaney shook Robert's hand.

"We're going to search the grounds first, then we'll fingerprint her room. Dr. Worth, is there anyone who would have an interest in this child—anyone that would stand to gain from abducting her?"

Marie gasped. "You mean—kidnapping?"

Robert's stomach tightened. Up to this minute he had not said the word even in his head. "Marie, is everything covered for first shift?"

"Yes." She answered with a clear note of pride in her voice. "Everyone's called home and worked it out. We're all staying."

"Thank you. I hate to ask you to do this, but would you please get the schedules and call the kitchen staff and housekeeping, O.T., and P.T.—anyone we can do without for a few hours? Breakfast may be a little late, but I think we can manage. We'll need Charissa to answer phones, I suppose. . ." He went through a mental list, then turned to the officer. "Let's go down to my office."

Jim Delaney's eyes widened as Robert told him who Annie's father was. "You're serious?"

"Yes. We've tried to keep it quiet. There are only eight staff and board members who have been in on it, and I trust every one of them implicitly."

"I'll need a list of their names, and all other employees, past and present. I need to know who has keys or access to them." The leather chair creaked as he leaned forward, holding a clipboard in both hands. "Dr. Worth, what's your gut feeling here? Is there any chance she just slipped out?"

"I don't think so. The doors are always locked at night, and she's a tiny girl; I don't think she could open a door on her own anyway."

"Is there anyone that comes to mind with a motive for taking her—anyone with a score to settle, who quit recently or was fired, anyone who talked about money problems? What about her mother, could she have changed her mind? How about Roman Slayder himself? Was he afraid he wouldn't get custody?"

"Annie's mother is voluntarily relinquishing her rights. She's an alcoholic with serious health problems. From the information we got from Human Services, I think she knows she's incapable of caring for Annie. I don't know about Roman. They're doing a home study on him and we were told we'd hear the decision today or tomorrow. I can't imagine he'd think he could get away with taking her."

Sergeant Delaney made a note on the clipboard, then

looked up. "But who has he told? And who's watching him? How much do you suppose he's worth? Several million maybe? There are a lot of opportunists in the world, Dr. Worth."

Robert ran his hand through his hair. "Annie is so trusting, she'd go with anyone when she's awake, but she's an ornery little bear when you wake her up. I can't imagine a stranger walking in here and carrying her out without a fight!"

Sergeant Delaney nodded. "Unless they drugged her, or unless it was someone she knew and trusted. . ." The knots in Robert's stomach hardened. There was something he had to tell the sergeant.

Just as he finished, David appeared at the door. Robert introduced the two men and David sat down. As Robert filled him in, David clasped his hands together and his knuckles whitened. Sergeant Delaney asked David several questions about the early resistance to the Sparrow Center, then sat back in his chair. "Tell me about your sister, Mr. Stern."

The slight widening of David's eyes told Robert that the implications in the questions had shocked him. "Paige would never. . .could there have been a lack of communication, Robert? Maybe she left you a note or thought it had been arranged. . ."

"David, I agree that this would be totally out of character for her, but we have to try to be objective. Annie was sound asleep at the 3:00 bed check. No one broke in, no one heard her cry. I can't by any stretch of the imagination picture Paige as capable of this, but—"

Shaking his head slowly, David finished the sentence for him. "But we can't deny that she does have a motive."

eighteen

At 7:30 A.M., Charissa walked in with a stack of computer printouts and a pot of coffee. "Time sheets, job applications, employee evaluations, volunteer lists. . . everything I could think of that might help."

Separating a stack of foam cups, Robert said, "You're a wonder, Charissa. Thank you."

David hung up the phone and shook his head while taking the cup Robert offered him. "There's no one at The Gallery yet and Brant doesn't answer his phone or his pager. He has the day off but his boss said he usually keeps his plectron and his beeper on all the time. I called the airport—his helicopter and plane are still there and they haven't heard from him."

Sergeant Delaney took the pen out of his mouth. "You think this McCourt is with your sister?"

"I don't know what to think anymore," David answered. "I drove out to his house before coming here. His truck was sitting in the driveway, but the Jeep wasn't there—not that I expected it to be." David rapped his fist on the arm of the chair. "I know what this looks like, but everything in me says there's a logical explanation. Paige is impulsive, but not foolish. I could see her suddenly deciding to take Annie somewhere overnight, since this may be her last chance, but. . ."

Sergeant Delaney raised one eyebrow and voiced David's own question. "In the middle of the night?" David shook his head. He'd run out of explanations. "Does she have a key?" the sergeant asked.

"No," Robert answered, "she's only a volunteer. But she could have had one made. I loaned her a key the night Roman was here."

David ran his hand over his face, trying to erase the fear and the incredible sadness that was washing over him. The evidence was getting stronger by the minute. "She has Hailey's keys," he said quietly. Addressing Robert he said, "With the baby and the wedding there's been so much going on. When she talked to me about wanting to adopt Annie, I honestly didn't take her very seriously. I really thought it was something that would pass. You talked to her about Roman; could she possibly have been this obsessed with the idea?"

"She was upset, but—"

A patrol officer poked his head into the room. "We've searched the grounds, sir. Nothing."

Sergeant Delaney nodded and held out a piece of paper. "Run a check on this, then call the station and make sure every squad in the county has it." He looked at David, then Robert. "If we have no leads by tomorrow morning, we'll be contacting the FBI."

Robert nodded. "Will it be possible to avoid this becoming a media circus?"

"The case will remain sealed while under investigation, but I think it would be overly optimistic to think that it won't get out. Between your employees and the people around Mr. Slayder, something is bound to leak. Have you reached him yet?"

"Charissa is trying. She only has his lawyer's office number, and it's 4:30 in the morning in L.A." Almost to himself he said, "I wish Cody were here."

The buzzer on Robert's phone sounded. "Maybe she reached Roman," he said as he pushed the button.

"Mr. McCourt is here, Dr. Worth."

"Send him in!" The three men stood as Brant walked in the room. Robert and David spoke at the same time. "Where's Paige?" they asked in unison.

Startled, Brant looked from Sergeant Delaney, to David, and then to Robert. "What's going on? I went out to the airport and they said you were trying to reach me. I tried calling, but I got a busy signal."

Sergeant Delaney looked at Robert. "That's not good. We have to make sure at least one line is open all the time." Looking back at Brant, he said, "Mr. McCourt, come with me. I have a few questions to ask you."

An hour later Brant walked slowly back to Robert's office. Finding the door open, he went in and sunk into a chair next to David. His thoughts moved slowly through the fog of questions Sergeant Delaney had raised. He stared at the pen in Robert's hand. "I want to say she couldn't do it, but I can't."

Robert nodded and David whispered, "I know."

Silence filled the room until David asked, "Did she ever say anything to you? Did you think she was that desperate?"

"Every time the subject of Annie came up I gave her a lecture about listening to God and not to her feelings. But I should have listened to her! I should have been able to see how intense her feelings were. She said something before the wedding that I didn't take seriously—about hijacking a plane and flying away with Annie. I thought she was joking."

David stared at the phone, willing it to ring. "She'd call, though, wouldn't she? Even if she didn't want us to know where she was, wouldn't she know how worried we are?" He looked up at Robert, feeling more helpless than he had in years. "I thought I knew her. . ."

Almost imperceptibly, Brant nodded. "Me too," he whispered.

Just before nine o'clock, David got through to The Gallery. Brant stopped pacing when David hung up the phone. "She called in sick, right?"

"She called the assistant manager at her home last night and said something had come up and she needed the day off. That's all she said."

Brant walked back to the window, then pounded his fist into his hand. "I gotta get out of here. I'll go get some donuts or something."

He passed the nurses' station on his way to the back door. One of the nurses was rocking back and forth with a child on each hip, another nurse was power-walking down the hall with a tray of medicine cups. He hadn't been around long enough to know any of them by name. Looking at the name tag of the woman behind the desk, he said, "Mrs. Wassal, put me to work. I can rock babies or read stories, and I look great in a pink wig."

The frazzled look left Marie's face as she stood and put her hand on Brant's arm. "Bless you, son." She nodded toward the nurse's aide who was holding the two toddlers. "Darla could use some help. You can entertain those two or you can come with me and I'll show you where we keep the diapers."

Brant held out his arms for the toddlers.

ॐ

Taking one hand off the steering wheel, Paige took off her sunglasses and rubbed her eyes, then massaged the tightness in her left shoulder. Her eyes burned from tears and lack of sleep and her body ached with exhaustion. As she reached down and stroked the ear of the stuffed pink rabbit on the seat beside her, she glanced at the clock on the dashboard. It was Annie's nap time.

The sight of the county sheriff's car parked perpendicular to the highway on a tractor path leading in to a corn field startled her. Automatically, she stepped on the brake and watched the needle drop from 62 down to 55, hoping she hadn't been detected by radar. Less than a quarter mile after passing him, she heard the siren. Looking in her rearview mirror, she saw the lights, and even before she pulled over to the shoulder, tears were stinging her eyes once again.

"Can I see your driver's license, ma'am?" Her hands were slow to cooperate as she tried to unzip her purse. Finally, she handed it to him.

"This your car, ma'am?"

"No. It belongs to a friend."

"May I see the registration please?"

She fumbled with the latch on the glove compartment, but finally produced the blue and white paper. The officer inspected it, handed it back, and then bent down to look inside the car. Gesturing toward the pink rabbit on her lap, he asked, "Anyone else in the car?"

"No."

"You look upset. Something wrong, ma'am?"

Paige swiped at a tear. "Just a difficult day."

"Where you headed?"

"The Sparrow Center."

"I see. . .maybe I'll follow you and make sure you get there safely."

It took her three tries to get the right key, and all the

while the sheriff's deputy sat in his car, talking on his radio and staring at her.

❧

The hall was eerily quiet as Paige approached the empty nurses' station. Then suddenly David, Robert, and a police officer were walking toward her. The officer stepped out ahead of them, around the U-shaped counter, and took her by the elbow. "Miss Stern, come with me. I have some questions for you."

"What's wrong? David? Robert? What's wrong?"

David walked toward her, but Sergeant Delaney stopped him. David's hand dropped to his side. "We can't find Annie, Paige."

"What? What do you mean you can't find her? Why aren't you looking?" She continued to ask questions as Sergeant Delaney guided her toward the room that David had been using as an office. Before she walked in, she turned and saw Brant at the end of the hall, holding a little blond-haired girl, staring at her.

Sergeant Delaney pushed "record" on the small tape recorder and set it on the table between them. "Why did you come here this afternoon, Miss Stern?"

Paige held up the stuffed rabbit that by now was damp from the palm of her hand. "I was bringing this to Annie. She pulled the ear off her old one and I promised I'd get her a new one."

"When did you last see Annie?"

"Three days ago. Tuesday afternoon I did chalk drawings with her and three other kids."

"You're sure you haven't seen her since then?"

"Yes, I'm sure!"

"Where have you been in the last twenty-four hours?"

Paige's mouth dropped. "What are you saying? I'm a suspect?" She started to laugh, then stopped herself. "Sergeant, I love Annie, I wanted to adopt. . .oh. . ." She sat back against the back of the chair. "I see how it looks." She sucked in a breath. "I needed time to think and pray, and I didn't want to be around when we got the results of Roman's home study, so I took off last night and drove up near Lake Delton. An artist friend has a cottage up there, so I called her. I had planned on staying all day, but I got some things worked out and I wanted to get back and spend some time with Annie."

"Did anyone see you?"

"Yes. Vicky Benton, she owns the cottage. I had to stop and get the key from her."

Sergeant Delaney asked several more questions, then laid a paper in front of her. "This is a list of the people who were working the night Mr. Slayder was here. Other than these, have you heard anyone talking, do you have any idea if anyone else knows who Annie's father is?"

Paige shook her head. Chewing on the end of his pen, Sergeant Delaney switched off the tape recorder. "I'm sorry we had to put you through this. I'd like you to stay here at the Center while we check out your story. There are no charges yet, Miss Stern, but I have to tell you honestly that, at the moment, you're the only lead we have."

Paige walked numbly into Robert's office and fell into David's arms. She was just starting to explain where she'd been when they heard the phone ring at the reception desk. Charissa's voice came over the speaker phone. "Dr. Worth, line two. He won't give his name."

Robert looked from David to Paige, then picked up the phone. "This is Dr. Worth."

"Tell her Daddy he can have her back when we get a hundred thousand dollars. I'll call back in the morning."

Robert repeated the message to David and Paige, and David asked, "Did you recognize the voice?"

"No. He had an accent; Puerto Rican I think, but it wasn't familiar."

Several minutes later, Sergeant Delaney joined them. "It was too short to trace, but we got it on tape and we know he's calling from a car phone. It's a start."

When Paige walked out of the office, Brant was leaning against the wall waiting for her. "I heard," he said, putting his hand on her arm.

"I'm scared. She's so little."

"I know."

"Brant, did you think I had taken her?"

Brushing her hair back, he said, "All I could think about was how I'd given you pat answers and sermons instead of trying to understand you. I'm sorry."

"That was pretty evasive for someone who doesn't soft pedal things."

"Okay, I'll admit I thought it was possible that you were so upset that your emotions took over. I'm sorry." He touched his lips to the top of her head. "And I'm sorry I've been a walking proverb instead of a friend."

Paige squeezed his arm. "Find me a cup of coffee and I'll give you a second chance."

"Deal. They've got chocolate pie in the kitchen."

He started leading her down the hall, but Paige stopped suddenly and pulled away from him. "Pie! That's it! Marsella was here the night Roman was here! Marsella's from Puerto Rico!" Leaving a bewildered Brant, she ran off to find Sergeant Delaney.

nineteen

Sergeant Delaney returned to the Center after questioning Marsella for over an hour. David had gone home and Brant was helping in the kitchen. Paige, holding a fussy four-month-old, joined Sergeant Delaney in Robert's office.

Looking at Robert, the officer said, "Marsella was in the supply closet when you walked past with Roman. She heard enough of your conversation to figure out his relationship to Annie. She knew who he was because her stepson Luis has a poster of him in his bedroom that he uses for a dart board. Evidently he's a fan of some band that has a rivalry with Quaestor. Marsella couldn't wait to get home and tell him who she'd seen! The poor woman was devastated when I told her about Annie. Anyway, it just happens that no one has seen Luis or his girlfriend since yesterday. My guess is one of them sneaked in with Marsella's keys. No one seems to know whose car they've got, probably stolen, but I've got someone searching their apartment. We'll find them. Have you heard from Roman yet?"

"His lawyer finally called. Roman should be at LAX right now ready to fly to St. Louis. He has a concert there tomorrow night. The lawyer said he'd page him and try to have him call us before he left. He was wondering if Roman should fly directly here."

"We need him to get the money together, just in case,

but I imagine the lawyer can handle that. I don't think he should change any plans just yet; that would only create media attention. Both these kids are addicts. They're after the money, but there may be revenge involved, too, some perverted fan loyalty or something. Seeing their faces plastered on TV might make them feel like heroes. We don't need that." Looking over at Paige's pale face, he said, "Go home and get some sleep. Once again, I'm sorry we had to put you through so much."

Paige nodded and stood, running her cheek across the soft hair of the baby who was finally sleeping in her arms. Looking at Robert she said, "I'll be back in the morning to help with breakfast. If anything comes up I'll be at David and Karlee's. I don't want to be alone tonight."

❧

Saturday morning dawned hot and hazy. Stepping out of the air-conditioned Jeep, Paige hit a wall of air almost too heavy to breathe. As she reached the front of the Sparrow Center, she caught a glimpse of a white paneled truck in the back parking lot.

Charissa ran to unlock the door for her. Several feet behind her stood the sheriff's deputy who had stopped her the day before. "Good thing you came to the front door," Charissa said. "There's a reporter and a cameraman out back."

"I guarantee there'll be a lot more before long," the deputy added.

Paige shook her head in frustration and walked across the lobby. Robert's door was closed so she headed for the dining room. The few people she passed made attempts at smiles or greetings, but the tension in the air was palpable.

At just after ten o'clock, she stood by Robert's desk, staring at the phone that he had just set in her hand. She watched his back as he left, closing the door partway, leaving her to talk to Roman alone. Lifting the receiver, she said hello and listened as he said, "I'll be heading out of here right after the concert tonight, but I wanted to talk to you before anyone else does. I just found out this morning that I've been granted custody." He paused a minute to give the news time to sink in. "I'm sorry to have to tell you this now."

Paige nodded, but it took her a minute to find her voice. Finally she said, "Right now I just want her to be safe."

"After she. . .comes home. . .I want to talk to you. I want to do this gradually, for all of us. I'd like your help."

"All right."

"Paige?"

"Yes?"

"I'm praying for Annie."

"I am too," Paige whispered. Thunder rattled the pane of glass in front of her. She hung up the phone and leaned her shoulder against the window frame. The black clouds rolling in from the west announced the coming rain, and the creeping darkness seemed a fitting atmosphere.

Turning to pick up her coffee cup from Robert's desk, she saw Brant standing in the doorway. She didn't pick up the cup; the look in his eyes as he walked toward her stopped her, stopped everything, including the storm of emotions in her head. In the next instant, she was in his arms, sobbing.

With one hand pressed against her back and the other on her head, he held her to him, stroking her hair, then resting his head on top of hers. When she stopped crying, he pulled her hair away from her face and lifted her chin. Softly, he ran his lips across her forehead, then touched them gently to her lips. "What happened while you were gone? Something's different."

Resting her head against his chest, she said. "I found my first love. I walked and I prayed and I cried and I finally let go. God is in the pilot's seat again."

Brant prayed a silent thank You and whispered against her hair, "'Sometimes it hurts when God makes you real, but it's worth the pain.'"

Instantly, he felt her stiffen against him. Drawing a sharp breath, he pulled his arms away from her. He had said it to himself so many times that he had forgotten where it came from. She took a step back and stared at him, her face turning red, her eyes wide with shock and blazing with anger.

"That's it! That's it! That's how you knew so much about me! Somehow, you read my letters to Gavin!" One hand flew to her mouth, then fell away. "Those were private letters. . .did he give them to you or did you sneak them?" She stared at him. "And then not to have told me? All this stuff about feeling like you knew me, all this talk about being 'real' friends—real friends don't lie, Brant!"

Pushing past him, she headed for the door. Brant grabbed her arm and held her. "Look at me."

She turned, glaring at him through her tears. "There are some things I should have told you," he said, "but I haven't lied to you since—"

"Then what do you call it? All this time of acting like you could read my thoughts! Were you just some kind of voyeur, getting your kicks out of reading someone else's mail? Did he post my letters on the bulletin board at the airport? I suppose it was a group effort, huh? Did you all work together, making up stuff for him to write?"

"No one else read your letters."

"You did!"

He let go of her arm. "Yes, I read them. But I was the only one." He paused, looking down at the floor. "Gavin never read them."

"What?!"

"Gavin never wrote to you. I did."

Paige felt like she'd been slapped. "I don't. . .understand."

"Sit down." She dropped to the couch and he sat next to her. "Gavin had your first letter in his pocket one day when he came in for a flight lesson. He hadn't even opened it. He was dating two other girls at the time he went out with you—all he ever talked about was his conquests, so I heard all about you. I know this hurts, Paige, but I need to defend myself a little, and I can't do that without telling you all of it. Gavin called you a 'pretty little prude.' He had no interest in investing in a long-distance relationship. He threw the letter at me and said, 'Here, you can have her.' "

Paige turned away, her face burning. Brant continued. "Please keep in mind that I wasn't a Christian at the time. I read the letter and I was intrigued. All those little sketches you'd drawn around the borders, and the way you described your roommate and your professors. . .I wrote to you just for fun that first time. I was living in an apartment over the old drug store and getting my mail at the post office at the time, so it was easy to give you my box number and tell you I used it because I didn't want my parents intercepting my mail. I guess my conscience wasn't completely seared because after that I was determined not to lie about anything else."

"Accept for one little detail!"

Brant ran his hand across his two-day beard. "I don't even know where to begin apologizing, Paige. Just let me try to explain how I saw it at the time. It started as a joke . . .at that time in my life I did anything that sounded fun, and I didn't give much thought to the consequences. I was in a restless stage; I didn't know what I wanted out of life. I was watching friends who were settling down with families or making big career moves and none of it seemed right for me. Always in the back of my mind were the things that Cody had told me for years, but I always shoved them back when they came to the surface. Then I got your letter and it was full of the excitement of the revival on your campus. You were so passionate! You talked about the freedom in being bound to Christ, about the joy of surrendering your will completely and letting Christ live in you. You were so open about how much you loved Jesus; your faith was so vibrant, so. . .tangible. You challenged me to search it out for myself and I did. I was determined to remain a skeptic until I was convinced, but I bought a Bible and I started studying."

Paige swiped at the tears that were spilling onto her lap. Brant looked down at the floor. "Every letter from you shed a little more light, but it did something else. It let me see inside you; your dreams, your secrets. . .By the time I realized what a horrible lie I was living, I was too scared of losing you."

Standing up, Brant walked to the window and stood with his back to her. "I was Gavin's flight instructor. I had no idea he was high when he came in for his first solo flight. For all I know, he may have taken something after he got in the plane. I was standing out on the tarmac, and by the time he was descending to land I could tell something was wrong. He was coming in way too fast. He'd done it so many times with me. . . ."

Paige watched his shoulders rise as he took a deep breath. Her mind was whirling; part of her wanting to comfort him, part wanting to run and never look at him again.

"Gavin's family blamed me. They said I should have known that he was taking drugs and I should never have let him go up. They wrote a few scathing editorials about me and airport policies in general. It was such a big deal in this little town, I was surprised that you didn't seem to know about it."

"No one knew I was writing to. . ." Paige put her hand over her face and closed her eyes, trying to make sense of what was happening. "Mom and I were here trying to help David after Shawna died. David was in his own world that first year. He didn't know Gavin, and I didn't think he even knew I'd gone out with him, but I guess he did, because he called me when he heard about the accident." She remembered the odd look David had given her on the day of Jordan's birth; he'd said something about how hard it must be for her to be with Brant. Her mouth twisted as she remembered; she'd assumed he must have been talking about what she'd thought was Brant's egotism.

Brant was silent for several long minutes. Then he said, "I called David. I just said that I was a friend of Gavin's and that you had met him while you were here and you needed to know about his death. I said it would be easier if you heard it from someone you knew. I was so afraid you'd come back for the funeral."

"I didn't know the Prentices; it wouldn't have made any sense for me to come back."

Leaning his forehead against the window, Brant said, "I left town three weeks after the funeral. The Prentices are very influential people in this town, and every time I walked down the street I felt like people were staring at me, like I'd been accused of first-degree murder. I went up to Canada and got a job with a search-and-rescue team. I kept up my Bible study and reread your letters until they almost fell apart. One day I was alone, flying into the sunset and watching the colors change and suddenly I just knew. I was cruising over the Canadian wilderness at 4,000 feet when I surrendered to Jesus."

He was quiet again for a long time, then slowly he turned. "I don't suppose it means anything to you right now, but I wouldn't have done it without you. You have no idea how many times I wanted to tell you, how many letters I wrote and threw away. It just seemed too hurtful. I knew you wouldn't ever want anything to do with me, and it seemed better to let you go on believing that the man you'd been writing to was dead. I never thought our paths would cross. I was in Canada, I figured you'd be home in Connecticut after graduation or working for a publisher in New York like you'd dreamed of. My grandmother had died and my grandfather was in a nursing home and didn't recognize me. I never thought I'd come back to Milbrooke."

Brant rubbed the back of his neck and said, "When my grandfather died he left the farm to me. I was totally unprepared for that. By rights, it should have gone to my dad, but he hadn't been much of a son. I just couldn't bring myself to sell the farm. After the funeral, I went back to Canada, but all I could think about was coming back here to start my own business. Cody had written me about the Sparrow Center and Hailey and the wedding. He mentioned Hailey's room-mate a couple times; I don't know how it happened that neither your name or David's ever came up. You have to believe that I never would have come back if I'd known you were here."

Rubbing her temples, Paige asked, "But why didn't you tell me when we met? I can understand—no, I can excuse your behavior before you were a Christian, but to continue in this charade while you're preaching to me about being in complete obedience to God! That's such blatant hypocrisy, I. . ." Dropping her hands to her lap, Paige rose slowly and turned toward the door.

"Wait. Please." He didn't make a move toward her, but his hands reached out, as if he could hang on to her from across the room. "What I did was wrong, but I need you to understand why."

Paige turned back, but kept her eyes on the window behind him, not trusting herself to look at him. "That whole year we were writing. . .it was strange, feeling like I knew you so well, and not knowing what you looked like. But I never asked you for a picture 'cause I didn't trust myself." He looked past her and said quietly, "I told myself that you can fall in love with a face, but not with words on a piece of paper." He sighed and ran his hand through his hair again. "Seeing you was like. . .like being hit by lightening or something. Suddenly there was this beautiful face to put with the words, but you were so different than I had imagined. Maybe I'd always pictured you in a white robe with a halo." For a brief second, he smiled. "All the time we were at David and Karlee's, I studied you. You talked about shopping in Paris, working at this fancy gallery, and buying a new car. . .Something was missing. It wasn't that I expected you to say 'Praise the Lord!' with every breath, but it sounded like you were filling your life with everything but God! You weren't real anymore! I wanted you to see how you'd changed and what you'd lost; I wanted to help you the way you'd helped me. I kept thinking that if we just had a little more time together before I told you, you'd see."

"A noble reason for deceit," Paige said sarcastically. "The end doesn't justify the means, Brant."

He lifted his hands just slightly, palms up, as if ready to begin a defense, then closed them into fists and nodded. "I know." He started to turn away, then stopped. "Only the name was a lie, Paige."

She stared at him, then turned, once again, to the door. This time, he let her go, but to her back he said, "I was wrong about one other thing. You can fall in love with words on a piece of paper. The face just made it sweeter."

twenty

The rain began while she was waiting for Charissa to unlock the glass door so she could leave. It fell in large, heavy drops that dotted the pavement and painted it a darker black.

When she reached the Jeep, the paneled truck pulled around the corner and a woman jumped out and ran toward her, then from the other side of the building came a man in a khaki jacket followed by a cameraman with an umbrella shielding his camera as he ran. Paige unlocked the car door and got in, slamming it just as the woman began shouting questions at her.

As she drove, her thoughts flowed in senseless circles, keeping time to the windshield wipers. Annie was lost, somewhere in the storm. Gavin was dead, but it didn't matter anymore, not to her. She had never really known him. Brant had lied to her, but in a way Brant was Gavin, or at least he was the person she had believed to be Gavin. Brant knew her secrets. . .He could read her like a book, but she couldn't trust him. Roman needed her help, but he was taking Annie away from her. But first they had to find her; she was lost, somewhere in the storm. . .

A strange thought came to her and she wondered why it hadn't hit her while she was talking to Brant. She almost laughed out loud at the irony: She was the too-perfect girl, the saintly legend who had led Brant to the Lord. She was the girl she'd been so jealous of!

She pulled into the driveway, but didn't get out. The house was empty and she didn't want to go in. The rain beat hard against the roof and sheeted on the windshield, blurring the edges and corners of the barn. Reaching in the back seat, she grabbed her hooded sweatshirt and slipped it on, then unplugged her cell phone and stuck it in the pocket.

The rain was cool on her face. Head down, she walked toward the road, watching the water cut through sand and stones, carving out miniature rivers at her feet. She had to think, she had to pray.

Father, none of this makes sense, but I'm not asking for an explanation. I've come back to You and I don't want to turn away again. I don't need to understand, but I need to know what to do. Please don't let my anger keep me from hearing You. My pride is hurt, but I have no right to pride. I know that I have to forgive Brant, but what then?

In the middle of the road she stopped and looked up, then closed her eyes. Her hood fell off and the rain soaked her hair and ran down her neck. She felt her sweatshirt grow heavy and her shoes fill with water, yet she stood, listening. What she heard, mingled with the sound of the rain battering the gravel, were Brant's words. "Only the name was a lie, Paige. . ."

The letters were in the storage area behind her closet. She ran back, unlocked the front door, and ran up the stairs, not taking the time to get out of her wet things. At the bottom of a box filled with sketch pads and photo albums were a year's worth of questions and reflections in white envelopes. Sitting on the floor of the walk-in closet, she pulled the first letter from the bottom of the stack, but as she bent to read it, her wet hair fell over her face. Spotting a headband in a basket behind the door, she pulled her hair back, away from her face.

She read out loud, but it was Brant's voice she heard. When she got to the end of the third letter, she noticed that he had signed it simply "me." After the second letter, the name Gavin never appeared. Somehow, that made it easier to erase him from the picture completely. So much fell into place as she read. Now she knew why her questions about his work and sports and family were always ignored. Now she knew why he had never called even though she'd told him he could. As the stack got smaller, her knowledge of Brant McCourt grew. It was as if she had started with a pencil sketch and then gradually added color. Though he had given none of the details of his life, he had given her bits and pieces of himself with every page.

She dialed the Sparrow Center on her cell phone as she walked out of the closet. Charissa answered with her usual cheery voice, as if nothing was different today. Paige asked to speak with Robert, and when he answered she asked if there was any news.

"Nothing yet."

"Is Brant still there?"

"No, he went home right after you left. Paige, I saw you run out. I wanted to talk to you after you talked to Roman. I'm worried about you."

"I'm okay, Robert. Annie's in God's hands and so am I."

❧

It was still pouring when she knocked on Brant's back door. He came to the door barefoot, in jeans and a white T-shirt. His hair was damp, as if he'd just showered and hadn't combed it yet, and he still had a two-day beard. The look on his face told her she was the last person he'd expected to find at his door. It took him a moment to respond, then, without a word, he opened the screen door for her.

Paige walked into the kitchen. It was more cluttered than she'd seen it the first time, but, she noticed, it was an organized mess. Dishes were stacked in the sink and papers piled on chairs, but they were neat piles. She glanced at the refrigerator. It was plastered with magnets holding scraps of paper: grocery and to-do lists, his work schedule and phone numbers—all in very familiar handwriting. Now she knew why he'd scrambled to take them off—and why he'd stenciled the invitation to The Greenhouse.

She turned to face him and wished she'd thought ahead about what she was going to say. He held out his hand. "Can I take your jacket?"

Paige looked down and saw the water dripping onto the chipped linoleum beneath her. She unzipped it, pulled the phone out of the pocket, and struggled out of it. "I'm sorry," she said, pulling off her wet shoes and turning to look for a paper towel.

"You're soaked through," he said, taking her jacket. "Come on, I'll get you something dry."

She followed him into the room with the magnolia wall paper. Two clothes baskets of folded clothes were sitting on the bed. He pulled out a towel and a pair of sweat pants, then opened the closet door and said, "Why don't you just help yourself to. . .whatever you need. The bathroom is the next door down the hall. I'll go heat up some coffee." He stared at her for several seconds with no expression in his tired eyes, then walked out, closing the door behind him.

She pulled a flannel shirt from the closet and the basket

of dark clothes provided gray socks, a navy T-shirt, and a pair of plaid boxer shorts. She held them up to her and giggled nervously. They would do. Taking the clothes into the bathroom, she peeled out of her wet things, dried off, and put on Brant's clothes. Only then did she look in the oval mirror above the sink. The only signs of make-up left on her pale face were the black streaks beneath her eyes, making her look like a backup singer for Quaestor. Turning on the water, she wet the corner of her towel and did the best she could to remove the mascara. She found a brush in an open drawer and worked through her hair, then, as an afterthought, put the headband back on.

Brant was facing the stove when she came in. Paige stood by the table, feeling like a little girl waiting to be told what to do next, but knowing that the first words had to be hers. He had done his apologizing, it was up to her to accept it.

He turned around, a brown mug in each hand. A hint of a smile flickered on his face when he saw her, but disappeared as quickly as it came. He set the cups on the table and motioned for her to sit down. Once again, she lifted his Bible and the devotional book and set them on the table.

Picking up the mug, she hugged it between her hands, looked out at the rain through the parted pink curtains, and said, "I read your letters over." She didn't know where to go from there, but she felt no need to fill the silence until she was ready. Finally, she said, "It was always hard trying to hear Gavin's voice when I read them; it never quite seemed to fit. But yours did." She took a sip of coffee, feeling the warmth spread down through her chest, then turned to face him. "Brant, I'm not sorry that it was you I shared my secrets with."

As her words wrapped around him, he reached out, took the cup from her hands and set it on the table. "Come here," he whispered, taking her hands and pulling her out of her chair and onto his lap. Closing his arms around her waist, he kissed her. "I've been wanting to do that for a long time," he said.

She smiled at him. "You haven't known me for a long time!"

He laughed. "I've known you for six years, girl."

Just as he kissed the tip of her nose, the phone rang. Paige slipped off his lap and Brant walked to the phone. "It's Delaney!" he whispered, pointing to the phone on the desk in the living room. Paige ran and picked it up.

". . .somehow they got through to Roman at his hotel. They want him to deliver the money personally at eleven o'clock tonight, knowing full well he'd have to bow out of his concert to get back here by then. Roman didn't want to risk being seen at the airport, so he rented a car. He can get to them by eleven, but that doesn't give us time to brief him and. . .get things ready on our end. Can you fly down and get him?"

"Of course." Brant looked out the window and saw, gratefully, that the rain had almost stopped. "If I take the helicopter I can bring him straight to the Center. Find me a place to land." He grabbed Paige's phone from the counter and pushed a button. "I'm taking Paige with me. I'll give you her cell phone number. If I haven't heard from you first I'll call you from the airport."

After hanging up the phone, he grabbed two jackets off a chair with one hand and Paige's wet shoes with the other. Staring into her fear-filled eyes, he said, "We'll have her back tonight."

twenty-one

They had been in the air, heading southwest, for less than five minutes when the call came in from Kip at the airport. "Brant, do you have medical equipment on board?"

"Just my trauma bag."

There was a long pause, and then, "That'll do. I have Sergeant Delaney on the phone. There's a medical emergency and he wants you to head for the old tile factory."

"Okay, I'm turning. What's this about?"

"A three-year-old girl—he says you'll know who it is—head injuries. She's bleeding heavily and hysterical, but the guy who has her refuses to take her to the hospital. They want medical help on the spot."

There was another long pause and Brant glanced at Paige. Her eyes were wide and her hand was covering her mouth. Kip's voice crackled over the radio again. "They won't give an exact location. You're looking for a car parked off the road with a red shirt on the roof. As soon as you see them, give me directions. Delaney will have squads close but out of sight. He says they may be armed and you should both get out with your hands up and let them see you're not armed."

Several minutes passed and Brant pointed. "I see it! In a clearing a quarter of a mile straight south of the lake, southeast of the crossroads. Tell Delaney I've got the cell phone with me if he wants to talk to me after we get on the ground!"

He set down in the middle of the field and took off his headphones and unfastened his seat belt, motioning for Paige to do the same. He pulled his trauma bag from behind the seat and put the cell phone in the pocket of his jeans. They got out and walked slowly toward the car. Brant held his trauma bag over his head in one hand. They were about thirty feet from the car when the driver side door flew open and a boy about eighteen jumped out.

"Stay there!" he yelled. Pulling a gun from behind his back and waving it at Brant he said, "Just her! Hand her the bag and you get over there where I can see you!"

"She's not trained!"

"Just send her with the bag!"

"She won't know what to do! I'm not armed, let me at least examine the girl!"

"No way! How do I know you're not a cop?"

"How do you know she's not a cop?" Brant yelled. To Paige, he said softly, "He's scared out of his mind and probably stoned. We're not going to reason with him. They've got a phone, call me on it and I'll tell you what to do."

"Brant, I can't do this. . ."

"Yes, you can. I'll talk you through it."

The boy turned the gun on Paige. "Start moving!"

"I can't do this!" she shouted.

"You're going to have to, lady, I don't trust him."

Brant held out the bag. "Annie needs you," he said. "Put on gloves before you touch her, then call me; I'll talk you through it," he repeated.

Her legs felt like lead as she started across the muddy, rutted field. When she got within ten feet of the car, she could hear Annie crying. The boy yelled and the passenger door opened. A young girl with short, dyed black hair and thick makeup was holding Annie in the front seat. The boy cursed. "Get over there and do something!"

Paige took two steps and he yelled again. "Wait! Bring the bag here first. Set it on the hood." He felt through the bag with one hand, never taking his eyes off Brant. The gun shook in his other hand. From the bag he pulled a pair of scissors and set them on the car, then handed the bag back to her, following her to the open car door.

Paige set the bag on the ground, opened it, and tore open a pair of gloves. Annie was only whimpering now. Her feet dangled limply over the girl's right arm, her eyes were closed, and the girl held a dark brown towel against the side of her head. "Where is she hurt?" Paige asked.

At the sound of Paige's voice, Annie sat up and let out a cry, reaching for her. The towel fell away and Paige gasped and felt her arms and legs weaken and tiny jolts spread out from the small of her back. The left side of Annie's face was covered with blood. Her curls were matted to the side of her head and her left sleeve was soaked. Running behind the car, Paige bent over and vomited.

Wiping her face with her sleeve, she walked back and sank to her knees, holding her arms out to Annie. "It's okay, baby, I'm here now." Annie shivered in her arms and her cold fingers bit into Paige's skin as she clung to her. Sitting down on the wet ground so that Annie could sit on her lap, Paige said, "Show me where it hurts."

Annie pointed to the side of her head. As Paige pulled back the matted hair, another wave of nausea swept over her. She squeezed her eyes shut and forced herself to breath slowly. *Dear God, give me strength.* She handed the towel to the girl. "Hold this against her head. Does anything else hurt, Annie? Your back or your neck?"

"No. I wanna go home."

"Soon, honey, soon." Looking into the pale face of the girl who looked to be no more than sixteen, she said, "That man is a paramedic. I need to use your car phone to talk to him so he can tell me what to do."

The girl unplugged the phone and handed it to her. Touching Annie's arm, the girl asked, "Is she hurt bad?"

"I don't know yet." She looked into the vacant gray eyes that were outlined with thick black liner. "What's your name?"

"Tammy."

The boy cursed again. "Shut up! Are you stupid?"

Tammy flinched and anger flared in Paige, evaporating the weakness in her arms. She turned to the boy. "They already know who you are, Luis! You're not going to get away with this!"

Fear flashed on the boy's face and the gun wavered. "I'll get away with it if I take you with me!" He waved the gun at Brant. "Get back! Away from the chopper!" he yelled.

Paige's finger shook as she punched in the number of her cell phone. "Hand it to me!" Luis shouted. Brant answered and Luis said, "Just tell her what to do. Once she stops bleeding, we're leaving and we're taking the lady with us. Any cops follow and she's dead!" He handed the phone to Paige.

"Brant?"

"I'm right here. Is she conscious?"

"Yes."

"Okay. Tell me what you see."

"There's a big gash above her ear and there's blood everywhere. It looks bad, Brant." The strength she had felt just a minute before had left her at the sound of Brant's voice. A sob shook her.

"Take a deep breath, Paige. You can do this. Rip open a compress and apply pressure, then wrap bandages around any way you can. Just keep talking to her, it'll help her stay calm."

Paige set the bag on Tammy's lap. "Help me open these bandages, then hand them to me as I ask for them." Tammy complied, and then Paige asked for the roll of gauze. Her hands trembled as she pressed the square bandages firmly against the wound. "I bought you a new bunny," she said, her voice quavering. "When we get home you can have it." Annie nodded, then started crying again as Paige began wrapping the gauze around her head.

"Tell me what happened, Tammy."

"She was sleeping in the back seat. Luis was driving too fast; he always drives too fast. He saw a cop and turned hard. I thought we were going to tip over."

Luis pounded on the roof of the car. "Shut up! Just make her stop bleeding."

Again, Tammy flinched, but kept talking. "She fell off the seat. There's a lot of junk on the floor, bottles and stuff. I don't know what she got cut on."

Before Paige had finished wrapping the gauze, the bandages were beginning to turn red. Her heart began to pound and her vision blurred; she put her head down and picked up the phone. "It's soaking through!" she cried.

"That's okay. Head wounds bleed profusely even when they're not serious. Just keep adding bandages and applying pressure. Is she complaining of pain anywhere else?"

"No."

"Is she alert? Does she recognize you?"

"Yes."

"Okay, listen to me, Paige. I think she's going to be fine, but we have to make them think it's life-threatening. We have to scare them into letting us take her. Check her eyes with the mag light and tell me her pupils aren't reacting, check her pulse and tell me it's thready, check her reflexes. Make it dramatic. You can do it."

Paige nodded and weakly said, "Okay," then set the phone down. She took a few deep breaths and raised her head slowly. Putting her fingers on the side of Annie's neck, she found her pulse. It was fast, but strong. She picked up the phone. In a panicked voice, loud enough for Luis to hear, she said, "Brant, her pulse is weak and thready!"

"Check her eyes."

"Tammy, get the flashlight out of the bag." She shined the light into Annie's eyes and picked up the phone again. "They're not reactive!" She turned to Luis. "She's lost a lot of blood, and it looks like she's got internal bleeding. There's nothing I can do about that, we have to get her to a hospital now! Luis, you're already going to be charged with kidnapping, do you want to add murder to it? Do you want to spend the rest of your life in prison?"

Tammy looked up at him pleadingly. "Luis, please, this is enough, let her go! We can still get away."

Slamming his fist against the side of the car, Luis swore at her again and walked several yards away. Tammy looked at him, then back at Annie. Her hands clenched into fists. With one final glance at Luis she leaned forward and whispered, "I took the bullets out of his gun last night! I didn't want anyone to get hurt! Take her and get out of here!" she whispered.

Paige's arms closed tighter around Annie, but she didn't move. "What will happen to you when he finds out?"

"Nothing that hasn't happened before. Go!"

Her prayer was nothing more than two words. *Dear God* . . .As much as she wanted to run, for Tammy's sake, she couldn't. Looking to Tammy, she said, "Okay. Go over there and distract him!"

When Tammy left, she picked up the phone. "Brant, the gun's not loaded!"

"You're sure?"

Paige closed her eyes. Could it just be part of their plan? She took a deep breath. "Yes, I'm sure. Hang up and call Delaney!"

"All right. Pretend you're still talking to me."

Before she could answer him, Tammy and Luis walked back to her. The look in Tammy's eyes was one of disbelief. Luis yelled, "Get in the car, we're getting out of here."

Paige stood slowly, holding Annie as if she were a porcelain doll, and said into the dead phone, "What will happen if we move her?" Looking up at Luis, she said, "He says the slightest jarring could kill her. Do you want that on your conscience?"

"I'll put something on this guy's conscience!" He ripped the phone from her hand and shouted into it. "We're getting out of here and we're. . ." He shook the phone, held it to his ear again, then threw it at her, striking her arm. His face contorted in rage, and Paige turned and began to run. The gun clicked and out of the corner of her eye she saw Tammy grab Luis's arm and heard her scream as he slapped her. Brant was running toward Luis, and Paige heard the impact as he tackled him to the ground.

As she lifted Annie into the helicopter, the squad cars appeared and the last thing she saw before closing her eyes and giving in to tears was Brant running toward her.

❧

Paige was curled on a chair in the hospital corridor with her head on Brant's paramedic jacket and the leather aviator's jacket covering her. Sitting next to her, Brant was stroking her hair. Her headband sat on his knee. He nudged her gently as Robert came out of the room across the hall and she sat up.

"She's sleeping," Robert said. "She's exhausted and dehydrated, but that's all. She'll have quite a scar, but her hair should cover it." He looked down at Paige, still in Brant's blood-stained shirt and sweat pants. "So I understand we can't call you a wimp anymore."

Brant put his arm around her. "You should have seen her—a regular Florence Nightingale!"

Paige rolled her eyes. "I don't think Florence Nightingale ever threw up in a crisis!"

"That happens to everyone the first time! Now that you've got that behind you, I can hire you for my ambulance crew!" Robert laughed at the look on Paige's face. "You two go home. I'll keep you posted."

Pulling her to her feet, Brant asked, "Are you too tired to have dinner with me, Florence?"

❧

Paige wrapped a towel around her wet hair and slipped into her robe. Standing in the closet, she went through her summer dresses one at a time. Pulling out a black satin shift, she smiled, shook her head, and hung it back on the pole. She knew exactly what to wear. Walking back to the bathroom, she took off her ring and laid it on the counter, took only mascara and lipstick out of her makeup bag, then opened the medicine cabinet and took out a bottle of fingernail polish remover.

An hour later, she opened the back door. Brant was wearing a white shirt and a tie with his jeans. He took one look at her and started laughing. Loosening his tie and pulling it off, he said, "I guess I don't need this."

"What were you planning?"

"I thought I'd fly you to Racine; there's a place on the lake front that makes the best roasted grasshopper with ladybug sauce around."

"I can change."

"No you can't." He reached out and tugged at her ponytail, touched her tiny gold earrings, then let his gaze wander down to the white v-neck T-shirt, the faded jeans, and leather sandals. Tipping her chin with his finger, he said, "You look beautiful."

"I wanted you to know there's more to me than satin and pearls."

❧

Brant got in the pilot's side and turned to look at Paige. "Ready?"

"Yup." She smiled at him and grabbed the yoke, gripping it so tight her knuckles turned white.

"Haven't you learned anything through all this?" He put his hand on her arm and tugged. "Let go." When he finally pulled her hand free, he held it up and pointed to the white line on her little finger. "Your hand is naked," he said. "It needs something." He brought it to his mouth and kissed her ring finger.

"Is that what it needed?"

"No. It needs something. . .untraditional. . .something red maybe." He continued to stare at her hand.

"Now what are you thinking?"

"That I love you." He stroked his finger along the back of her hand. "And I was thinking about a Proverb Cody quoted to me a while ago."

Paige groaned. "Go on, Solomon."

" 'Who can find a virtuous woman? Her price is far above rubies.' " He kissed her finger again. "I found one, and I'm willing to pay the price."

Paige wiped a tear from her cheek, then leaned over and kissed him. "So, you think you'll like me better in jeans and rubies than satin and pearls?" she whispered.

"I like you in anything—as long as you're real."

"How long does it take to be real?"

"It takes a long, long time." He wrapped her in his arms and kissed her firmly. "But I'll talk you through it."

A Letter To Our Readers

Dear Reader:

In order that we might better contribute to your reading enjoyment, we would appreciate your taking a few minutes to respond to the following questions. When completed, please return to the following:

Rebecca Germany, Managing Editor
Heartsong Presents
P.O. Box 719
Uhrichsville, Ohio 44683

1. Did you enjoy reading *Far Above Rubies*?
   ❏ Very much. I would like to see more books
      by this author!
   ❏ Moderately
      I would have enjoyed it more if _____

   _____

2. Are you a member of **Heartsong Presents**? ❏Yes ❏No
   If no, where did you purchase this book?_____

   _____

3. What influenced your decision to purchase this
   book? (Check those that apply.)

   ❏ Cover   ❏ Back cover copy

   ❏ Title   ❏ Friends

   ❏ Publicity   ❏ Other_____

4. How would you rate, on a scale from 1 (poor) to 5
   (superior), the cover design? _____

5. On a scale from 1 (poor) to 10 (superior), please rate
    the following elements.

    ___Heroine   ___Plot

    ___Hero   ___Inspirational theme

    ___Setting   ___Secondary characters

6. What settings would you like to see covered in
    Heartsong Presents books?_____

    _____

    _____

7. What are some inspirational themes you would like
    to see treated in future books?_____

    _____

    _____

8. Would you be interested in reading other **Heartsong
    Presents** titles?   ❏ Yes   ❏ No

9. Please check your age range:
    ❏ Under 18   ❏ 18-24   ❏ 25-34
    ❏ 35-45   ❏ 46-55   ❏ Over 55

10. How many hours per week do you read? _____

Name _____

Occupation_____

Address_____

City_____ State_____ Zip_____

········· Presents ·········

Great Inspirational Romance at a Great Price!

Heartsong Presents books are inspirational romances in contemporary and historical settings, designed to give you an enjoyable, spirit-lifting reading experience. You can choose wonderfully written titles from some of today's best authors like Veda Boyd Jones, Yvonne Lehman, Tracie J. Peterson, Nancy N. Rue, and many others.

When ordering quantities less than twelve, above titles are $2.95 each.
Not all titles may be available at time of order.